MURDER AT THE BOMB SHELTER

A ROSA REED MYSTERY BOOK 3

LEE STRAUSS

NORM STRAUSS

Cover by Steven Novak

Cover Illustration by Amanda Sorenson

Library and Archives Canada Cataloguing in Publication Title: Murder at the Bomb Shelter : a 1950s cozy historical mystery / Lee Strauss. Names: Strauss, Lee (Novelist), author. Description: Series statement: A Rosa Reed mystery ; 3 Identifiers: Canadiana (print) 20200181300 | Canadiana (ebook) 20200181319 | ISBN 9781774090985 (hardcover) | ISBN 9781774090961 (softcover) | ISBN 9781774090978 (IngramSpark softcover) | ISBN 9781774090947 (EPUB) | ISBN 9781774090954 (Kindle) Classification: LCC PS8637.T739 M872 2020 | DDC C813/.6—dc23

ROSA REED MYSTERIES

IN ORDER

Murder at High Tide
Murder on the Boardwalk
Murder at the Bomb Shelter
Murder on Location
Murder and Rock 'n' Roll
Murder at the Races
Murder at the Dude Ranch
Murder in London
Murder at the Fiesta
Murder at the Weddings

1

Rosa Reed pedaled her Schwinn *Deluxe Hollywood* bicycle down the boulevard on another sunny Santa Bonita, California day. As she breathed in the sweet scent of sage and saline, she briskly rode down the slight incline toward *Ron's New and Used Cars*. Over the last few weeks, she'd ridden by often, but today her heart fluttered with excitement as she approached the business establishment.

Yesterday, while heading home from a short shopping trip with her brown tabby kitten, Diego—who rode in the front basket with his fuzzy face into the wind—she'd spied a new arrival on the car lot. She'd simply *had* to stop for a look. That polo-white, two-door 1953 Chevrolet Corvette Roadster convertible with red-leather interior had gripped her imagination, and at that moment, Rosa had fallen in love.

One of only three hundred made that year, the automobile, with its serial number of 76, was already considered a collector's item. Rosa had slid into the red-leather seat with Diego safely tucked into her satchel. When she'd revved the engine, the frame rumbled, and the powerful sound roared through the tailpipe, causing her to smile mischievously.

With the top down, she'd test-driven the vehicle, riding north onto the Pacific Coast Highway—a warm August breeze mussing her short brown hair. She'd allowed herself a moment of thrill when she pressed harder on the accelerator. *My mother would love this car*! The thought made her laugh out loud as she thundered past the city limits sign, swirls of dust whipping in her disappearing wake.

Upon returning to the lot, Rosa had immediately phoned her Aunt Louisa, the matriarch of the Forrester mansion, to arrange for temporary financing until she could get the money wired from the London bank that held her trust fund.

"I'm part of the Forrester family," she'd told the dealer. "I'll be back tomorrow if you'd be kind enough to hold it for me."

By the look of respect at the mention of the Forrester family name—and perhaps a little fear, after all, Aunt Louisa's reputation in the town was formidable—the dealer promised to hold it.

Now, as Rosa signed the papers for ownership and registration, anticipation rushed through her. The days that lay ahead of her! Her recent decision to stay in Santa Bonita and set up a private investigation office instead of returning to her job as a police officer in London was further cemented by the purchase of this car.

"You don't mind stowing my bicycle for a day or so . . ." Rosa said, her voice a lively lilt. ". . . until I can arrange for it to be picked up."

"Not at all, Miss Reed," the dealer said with a firm handshake and a grin as sparkling as Santa Bonita bay.

Minutes later, Diego safely ensconced in her large satchel, Rosa pointed the Corvette toward the business district. She'd remembered to bring a silk headscarf, the same pink color as her lipstick—her mother would approve—so her hair stayed neatly in place. A pair of gray-and-green Polaroid tortoiseshell sunglasses sat on her nose, and she steered her new steed along the roadway with gloved hands.

She congratulated herself for staying in the right-hand lane. Rosa had learned to drive in America during the war years when she'd been shipped out of London to the safety her Aunt Louisa had offered. Shifting from her inclination to drive on the left was like riding a bike. Having a steering wheel on the left-hand side, rather than the right, helped with reorientation.

Shortly afterward, Rosa parked her Corvette along the curb in front of an office building. Now, standing by the front entrance, she paused to admire her new car before stepping inside. Diego meowed softly from his spot inside the designer pink-and-yellow striped satchel that matched Rosa's outfit. Her rose-and-yellow polka dotted swing dress had a row of large white buttons running down the bodice and a white patent leather belt accentuating her narrow waist. She'd finished off the outfit with yellow heels, the ankle straps tied into dainty bows. Rosa had discarded her first ragged satchel, a temporary accessory used when the need was urgent, and had accumulated several new cat-carrying bags to replace it.

Her second-floor office was the last door on the left down the wide carpeted hallway that ran past several law firms and busy accounting businesses. A large window at the end of the hall overlooked the street below. Rosa stepped back to regard the freshly painted lettering on the frosted glass that made up the upper half of the oak door—*Reed Investigations*.

A few days ago, when the sign painters had put the final touches on the lettering, she had snapped a picture of it to send to her parents. She knew they would burst with pride at the sight of her name on the door. Rosa had spent a large part of her youth working with her mother, Ginger Reed, at the office of *Lady Gold Investigations* and credited that time for her apparent aptitude for sleuthing. She'd also learned from her work as a female member of the London Metropolitan Police. As her father, Basil Reed, a superintendent at Scotland Yard, liked to say, the apple didn't fall far from the tree.

Rosa slid the key into the lock, opened the door, and gently put her satchel down on the blue, padded cushions of the teakwood, Danish-style sofa that served as reception area seating. Diego immediately jumped out to explore the room.

With Gloria's help—her cousin had decided to study interior design, and Rosa couldn't help but wonder how long this particular passion would last—Rosa had outfitted the office to match the Spanish mission design of the building. Brightened by sunlight streaming in from a large window, the room had an impressive view of Santa Bonita's business district. Green, leather-padded chairs circled a Spanish-mission-inspired coffee table. Adjacent to that was a matching desk. A set of shelves lined a portion of one wall, which Rosa planned to fill with books.

She'd already ordered certain law reference books and other resources such as textbooks on modern forensics and police investigative practices. A few mysteries and detective novels she'd picked up at the local bookstore lined one of the shelves along with a set of history encyclopedias and certain literary works of famous authors like Mark Twain and Ralph Waldo Emerson.

Rosa wanted the office to have a comfortable and inspiring ambiance. A kitchenette at one end of the office featured a small range, refrigerator, and cupboards for dishes and minimal food storage. A cast-iron bistro table sat in the corner with two chairs, which suited the Spanish terra-cotta tiling on the floor.

An adjoining door opened to a darkroom, much like the one in her mother's office in London. Rosa had purchased an Argus 35mm camera, like the one she had used for her police work. Not only was she adept at using the camera, but she also did a fine job developing the photographs. It was much faster and easier than taking the film to a photograph processing lab.

Diego immediately curled up on a chair, while Rosa removed her sunglasses, scarf, and gloves and set them on a side table. Settling into her desk chair, she arranged her crinoline slip and her skirt then stared out of the window at the vehicles rumbling down the street.

Rosa's gaze settled on the recently installed black telephone, which seemed to mock her with its silence. For a moment, she felt a twinge of doubt. Had she been presumptuous in her decision to stay in California?

Who was she to think that her assisting the Santa Bonita Police would cause anyone to seek her out for private investigating? Not only was she not American (her English accent an instant giveaway), but she was also a woman. Two definite strikes against her when it came to competing for work. And then there was Detective Miguel Belmonte—her pulse raced a little at the thought of him.

The thought of returning to London made Rosa's stomach twist. The social circle belonging to the elite in London was small, and she wasn't ready to face her peers, or the tabloids who'd had a heyday after she'd abandoned her fiancé, Lord Winston Eveleigh, at the altar.

And there was Larry. Rosa and the assistant medical examiner, Dr. Larry Rayburn, had been on several dates since she'd given him her number back in June, and she found his Texas charm delightful.

Besides that, Aunt Louisa had made it clear that the Forrester mansion was Rosa's home for as long as she wanted to stay. While her cousin Clarence had been indifferent, Gloria had been ecstatic. "Maybe I should take up journalism after all. We could work together!"

"Who knows?" Rosa had replied, laughing. Her cousin's mind changed like the wind. "Anything is possible. Let's see what happens."

That seemed Rosa's motto these days. Let's see what happens, let the wind take the sails, or *que sera sera,* as she had recently heard Doris Day sing on the radio.

The shrill ring of the telephone, a sound she hadn't yet heard, startled Rosa. Who could it be? She hadn't even given out her number to anyone. Perhaps someone who'd seen the advertisement she'd placed in *The Santa Bonita Gazette*, but it had only come out this morning. This couldn't already be a client?

"Miss Rosa Reed from Reed Investigations." Rosa smiled to herself as she uttered the words for the first time.

"Hello, Miss Reed." The voice was throaty and female. "My name is Mrs. Gainer. I hope you can help me."

"I'll do my best, Mrs. Gainer," Rosa replied. "What is it that you need?"

"I have four brothers-in-law, and one of them, Dieter Braun, is a particularly odd character, you see. Every family has one of those, don't they?"

Rosa agreed, her mind going to Aunt Louisa and Grandma Sally. "Sometimes, more than one."

"Well, Dieter's been missing for four days, and I think he's in trouble." Mrs. Gainer's voice grew somber. "I think he's been kidnapped or...maybe even worse!"

2

Later that day, Mrs. Janet Gainer sat in a chair in front of Rosa's desk. Dressed in an expensive-looking taffeta dress and an exquisite lace and crinoline trimmed half-hat, Mrs. Gainer had light-brown hair and an open, honest face. Fine lines around expressive blue eyes had Rosa guessing that the lady was in her late forties, but possibly older. Women of means tended to age well.

Rosa removed a fresh notepad from her desk drawer along with her new Papermate ballpoint pen then stared across at Mrs. Gainer with interest. Mrs. Gainer's attention, however, focused on Diego, who licked a paw and drew it over his forehead.

"It appears now is as good a time as any for bathing," Rosa said.

Mrs. Gainer's expression, up-to-now rather serious, softened into a smile. "He's adorable. Can I hold him?"

"Certainly, though I warn you, Diego's rather naughty. A little fur ball of energy."

As was becoming typical, Diego had a way of making a liar out of Rosa. When Mrs. Gainer picked him up and placed him on her lap, he instantly purred while she stroked his back and tickled his ears.

"I grew up on a farm just outside of Jefferson, Iowa," Mrs. Gainer said with a note of pride. "We had at least a half-dozen cats at any given time living in our barn. As a little girl, I used to love going in there and playing with the kittens."

"I found him outside a bakery," Rosa said. "I couldn't resist."

"Oh, he's so adorable!"

Diego's eyes got sleepy as Mrs. Gainer stroked the stripy spot on his nose right between his eyes.

"When he wants to be," Rosa chuckled. "He can sometimes be a stinker." At least according to Aunt Louisa, who had rather had enough of Diego's antics. "He likes to gift my aunt with fur balls."

As she glanced up at Rosa, Mrs. Gainer laughed lightly. "You have an accent. Is it Australian?"

"No," Rosa replied. "I'm from London."

Rosa sensed that Mrs. Gainer was avoiding the

reasons for her visit and feared her potential client might be having a change of heart.

"Mrs. Gainer, you came to me because you were worried about your family member. Would you like to tell me more?"

"Yes, of course. You're new to Santa Bonita, so you're unfamiliar, I suppose, with the Gainer family."

Rosa knew the name. Like the Forrester clan, the Gainers were what Londoners might call the social elite.

"I've heard the name, but not much else."

"Yes, well, I'm stepping out of line by coming to you, and I'm sure I'll get my wrists slapped by my father-in-law."

Rosa kept up with the society columns of the local papers—an expedient way to become acquainted with who was who in Santa Bonita—and had learned that Mr. Orville Gainer, the patriarch, was a highly successful and wealthy businessman. Rosa's admiration for Mrs. Gainer went up several notches. It would take a good amount of courage to cross a man like that.

"The missing man you mentioned, can you tell me more?"

"Yes. I suppose I should back up a little. I'm married to Michael Gainer, the youngest of Orville Gainer's sons. The other is Walter, the eldest sibling. There are three daughters in between, Alice, Valerie, and Lillian, now deceased. She was married to Dieter Braun, who, obviously, is of German descent." Mrs. Gainer glanced away, looking rueful. "You'll learn this about my father-in-law sooner than not, so I might as well get the unpleasantness out of the way. Orville Gainer doesn't have a lot of patience with foreigners."

Rosa hummed her understanding. Prejudice wasn't an uncommon societal blight, and Rosa had encountered it often in her line of work. It was a problem on both sides of the Atlantic. Especially, due to the two world wars, toward German immigrants.

"Has anyone reported Mr. Braun's disappearance to the police?"

Mrs. Gainer, still petting Diego, paused mid-stroke. He nudged her with his nose, and she resumed. "This is why I've come to you, Miss Reed. My family doesn't want to get the police involved."

"Why not?"

"What I tell you is in confidence, right?"

Rosa nodded. She was only compelled to go to the police if she came across information that could put another person in harm's way.

"The Gainer family business practices aren't always on the up-and-up. I doubt anyone with this kind of money has come into it in purely honorable ways."

As Rosa scribbled notes, sudden dizziness overtook her. Mrs. Gainer gathered Diego into a close embrace with one arm and gripped the desk with the other. She locked eyes with Rosa and announced, "Earthquake."

Rosa's blood rushed to her cheeks as she grabbed ahold of the desk. The second one in six days! Until last week, she'd almost forgotten about this West Coast hazard.

Everything stilled, and Rosa released a nervous laugh.

Mrs. Gainer smiled in return. "You'll get used to it."

Rosa wasn't quite willing to concede to that. "We'll see." She took a moment to catch her breath then referred to her notes. "Your husband, Michael Gainer, does he share your concerns?"

"No. He works at one of Dieter's insurance companies and says it's normal for him to leave on extended business trips."

"So, why are you troubled about his absence?"

"Dieter is an odd sort. None of the family like him, but he and I get along." Mrs. Gainer's eyes grew sad. "We share the same weird sense of humor. His pet name for me is *Schatz,* which is a German endearment for treasure. I think he's lonely. He often tells me about his businesses and jokes that he puts up with Michael for my sake. He always tells me when he plans to leave town."

As if a fierce wind caused the building to sway

slightly, a rolling sensation crossed the room, causing the conversation to stop.

"Oh my," Rosa muttered.

"Aftershock," Mrs. Gainer said, a few seconds after the feeling subsided.

Rosa swallowed. "Indeed. Please proceed."

"As I've said, Dieter is peculiar. Besides his German heritage, the Gainers enjoy ridiculing him because he's always talking about secret government plots, alien abductions, and the threat of nuclear war."

Rosa held Mrs. Gainer's gaze. "Do you suspect foul play?"

Mrs. Gainer lifted a thin shoulder. "It seems disloyal to the family to say it, but yes, I do. Though I don't have any evidence to support my suspicions."

Rosa poised her pen over the notepad. "It would be helpful for me to know about the other family members."

"Of course." Mrs. Gainer shifted her weight and crossed her legs. "Walter is married to Patricia. Like Lillian and Dieter, they never had children. Alice married Frank Monahan and they have a son Colin, who's the same age as my son, Sidney. And Valerie married Leo Romano. They have a daughter, Debbie."

Rosa jotted the names down rapidly, then glanced up. "I know Mr. Braun has a habit of telling you about his comings and goings," she said, "but is it possible he simply forgot this time? Do you know if he has any friends he might be visiting? Or maybe extended family?"

"Dieter didn't have a lot of friends here in California, and all of his relatives are still in Germany. And no, I don't think he forgot."

"How about any favorite getaway spots?"

"He owns a cabin out on Lake Fairbanks. It's a forested area in the hills east of here. Thinking that's where he might be, I drove out there yesterday, but the door was locked. I peeked in the windows, but it didn't look like anyone had been there for a long time."

"Does your brother-in-law have any health issues?"

Mrs. Gainer shook her head. "He's as healthy and physically fit as any fifty-eight-year-old man can be."

Rosa finished writing in her notepad then leaned back in her chair. "So just to confirm, you haven't told anyone that you are seeking to hire a private detective."

"No, not yet."

"To be honest, Mrs. Gainer, I am not sure how comfortable I am about taking on a case without the family's knowledge."

"I think that will change in a few more days when it becomes obvious Dieter is truly missing, and something has to be done. In the meantime, I have an idea about how you can meet the family without them necessarily knowing why."

. . .

Once Mrs. Gainer had left, Rosa picked up the phone receiver and dialed her friend Nancy. Good friends from the time Rosa had spent in high school in Santa Bonita, she and Nancy, then known as Nancy Davidson, had grown apart in the intervening eleven years. Rosa had come back to Santa Bonita, licking her wounds after her failed attempt at nuptials. Her relationship and subsequent engagement to Lord Winston Eveleigh had been birthed in crisis when Winston's sister Vivien, Rosa's dear childhood friend, had been murdered, a case that remained unsolved.

Happily, Rosa and Nancy's friendship had been renewed since Rosa had decided to stay in California.

"Hello, Nancy," Rosa said excitedly when her friend answered.

"Hiya, Rosa! What's up?"

"I got a client today."

"Oh, that's swell! What's the deal-i-o?"

"A missing person from an established family. I can't divulge the details, but it means I won't be able to come for dinner tonight."

Rosa could imagine her friend pushing her short honey-blonde curls behind her ear and wrinkling her ski-slope nose. "Oh, phooey. And I was going to make Swanson's turkey TV dinners."

"I do apologize."

"It's fine. I'll whip up something else for Eddie and the boys and save the Swanson's until you can come."

"Thanks for understanding."

"Hey, I want to hear all the dirt someday. You know I live vicariously through you."

Rosa made promises to that effect before hanging up. Collecting Diego, she headed back to the Forrester mansion. She had something to get ready for.

3

A white Spanish mission-style home that looked over several acres of gardens and a sprinkling of orange and lemon trees, the Forrester mansion rested on a knoll at the foot of the hills. An inviting kidney-shaped swimming pool, a tennis court, and the requisite lines of palm trees added the required luxuries.

It was home away from home, though nothing could ever replace Hartigan House in Kensington where Rosa had—outside of those four years during World War II—been born and raised. She'd never lived on her own, and she'd nearly moved onto the Eveleigh estate as Winston's wife. Rosa mused that she could move into her office if she wanted to live alone. It had the necessities to house her, but she'd miss the stimulation that a household of people—family and staff—

provided, not to mention the indulgence of the pool and family library at her disposal. Besides, her office would provide her an oasis of peace anytime she needed solitude.

Coasting past the front entrance, Rosa parked her Corvette in the six-car garage just as her cousin Clarence was leaving. He wore a sharp-looking cotton suit buttoned at the waist, a straw fedora, and brown leather saddle shoes.

"Holy smokes!"

Rosa grinned as Clarence's eyes flashed with envy. "Where did you get that?"

"I bought it this morning. Do you like it?"

Clarence scoffed. "If I wasn't on my way out, I'd demand you let me take it for a ride."

Rosa held the keys in the air and shook them. "Whenever you want."

"Golly, Rosa," Clarence filled his cheeks with air. "You really know how to tease a fella."

Rosa set her satchel on the ground, and Diego scurried into the house through a door that Clarence had left open.

She glanced back at Clarence. "Where are you off to?"

It was just a friendly question, and Clarence took it as one. "Picking up Julie to take her to the park for a couple of hours. Vanessa's getting her hair done."

Vanessa was Clarence's ex-wife, and Julie, their four-year-old daughter. The divorce caused strained relations between Vanessa and the Forrester clan, particularly with Clarence's mother—Rosa's Aunt Louisa—but Clarence did his best to make the most of a sad situation, especially where his daughter was concerned.

"Hey, Clarence," Rosa ventured as Clarence opened the driver's door to a red Thunderbird. "What do you know about the Gainer family?"

Clarence answered as he slid into the front seat. "Large, rich, powerful. Orville Gainer is a pompous donkey. They all are."

"I take it you don't get on?"

"Longtime rivalry between our family and theirs. Only room for one powerhouse at the top, apparently. We reigned there for years until Dad died." A shadow passed behind Clarence's eyes as he pinched his lips together. As the male head of the family, Clarence had found it difficult to fill his father's shoes, a task made doubly difficult since Aunt Louisa was bound and determined to wear them too.

Rosa said goodbye to Clarence and went inside to search for Diego. Her new pet had won the hearts of everyone except Aunt Louisa, so Rosa did her best to keep the two separated. Out of sight, out of mind.

She found him in the first place she looked, in the

kitchen with the housekeeper, Señora Gomez, who constantly pampered the cat with bowls of milk.

"Hello, Miss Rosa!" the housekeeper said with a bright smile. She patted Diego on the head. "I knew you were home."

"Diego let the cat out of the bag?" Rosa chuckled at her pun. After a second, Señora Gomez caught the joke and laughed.

"You're too funny, Miss Rosa. And you must be hungry, no? Mrs. Forrester and Miss Forrester are lunching by the pool. Would you like to join them?"

"That would be fabulous, Señora Gomez. Thank you. Do you mind if Diego stays with you?"

"He's always welcome." Señora Gomez had put a chair under the window where Diego could bask in the sun, far enough away from where she bustled about near the kitchen counters and appliances.

From a distance, Gloria and Aunt Louisa looked like sisters, each with trim figures and short curls pinned back behind the ears, except that Aunt Louisa's hair was dark, and Gloria had recently gone platinum-blonde. It was only when Rosa drew closer that the difference in ages became apparent. Her aunt had fine lines around shrewd eyes and tight lips, whereas Gloria's youthful expression was light with few worldly cares.

Gloria enthusiastically waved when she spotted Rosa. "Oh goody! Rosa's here."

Rosa pulled up a patio chair and joined Aunt Louisa under the shade of the umbrella. It was an annoyance that Rosa's fair skin burst into a bouquet of freckles when it met with the sun.

Aunt Louisa stared at her over the rims of a snazzy pair of cat-eye sunglasses that had white and red striped frames. "You were off early this morning," she said.

"I bought a car."

Gloria sat straight with renewed interest. "What?"

Aunt Louisa rolled her eyes. "We have a garage full of vehicles. You could've taken your pick."

"I do appreciate your generosity, Aunt Louisa," Rosa said. She'd made use of one of the vehicles, a two-toned yellow Chevrolet Bel Air, quite extensively. "But it's not the same as having one's own." Not only had Rosa felt compelled to let someone know every time she took the Bel Air, but she was also nervous about causing damage to the vehicle.

"What did you buy?" Gloria asked.

At that moment, Rosa spotted Señora Gomez, who arrived with a plate of food for her. She teased her cousin, "I'll show you after lunch."

"How enigmatic of you," Aunt Louisa said wryly.

Rosa held in a smirk. "I'll only say that I ran into

Clarence on my way in, and he loved it." Clarence was a connoisseur of luxury vehicles, and his opinion went a long way.

"My curiosity is unbearable!" Gloria said.

Lunch was a bowl of tomato soup paired with a deliciously greasy cheddar cheese grilled sandwich. Rosa thanked the housekeeper again before taking a bite.

Rosa watched with interest as Gloria shifted in her chair as if struggling with a bout of nerves.

"Is everything all right?" Rosa asked.

"I'm taking acting lessons."

Aunt Louisa dropped the book she was reading onto the patio floor. "Acting? You can't be serious. What is wrong with interior design?"

Gloria sighed. "I'm really only interested in designing rooms that I myself plan to dwell in. I find I'm quite bored with the process when it comes to dealing with strangers."

"You change your mind so fast that my head spins, dear," Aunt Louisa said.

Gloria raised her chin in indignation. "I refuse to settle until I find the perfect thing to devote my life to."

"I'm sure you can come up with something more fitting than acting."

"There's not a lot a girl can do," Gloria said, "and

acting is a perfectly respectable profession. I start classes next week."

Gloria's list of new pursuits was getting rather long, Rosa mused. Dancing, journalism, interior design, and now acting, or rather, a return to acting. Finding purpose in one's life was a matter of importance for most people, and Rosa was happy she'd found hers in police work, and now in private sleuthing.

"I'm sure you'll have a lot of fun," Rosa said.

Gloria shot her a look of contempt. "I'm not just doing it for fun."

"No, of course not, but you can still have fun anyway, can't you?"

Gloria threw her head back and laughed. "Of course, Rosa. And thank you for believing in me." With that, she shot her mother a look of rebuke, but Aunt Louisa simply picked up her book and started reading again.

Deciding now was a good time to change the subject, Rosa ventured, "What do either of you know about the Gainer family?"

Aunt Louisa frowned, and after a long pause said, "Why do you ask?"

"I've been invited to a party there," Rosa replied.

"Oh-oh," Gloria clapped her palms together. "Can I come?"

Before Rosa could make up an excuse to decline,

Aunt Louisa snapped, "Absolutely not!" She glared at Rosa. "And I would strongly suggest that you decline the offer as well."

"Why?" Rosa said, intrigued. This feud between families appeared to go deep.

"Orville Gainer is a chauvinist, that's why. He can't even make eye contact with me when I'm standing two feet in front of him."

"When is the party?" Gloria asked, apparently not sharing the same concerns.

"Tonight."

Gloria and Aunt Louisa both gawked then said simultaneously, "Tonight?"

Aunt Louisa added, "A late invite doesn't bode well. What brought this on?"

"An old friend of Aunt Felicia's happened to marry into the Gainer family." Felicia wasn't a blood relative, but Rosa had always used the endearment when referring to her mother's former sister-in-law. And though Janet Gainer had been to London, the two ladies had never actually met, but it was the cover story Rosa and Mrs. Gainer had agreed on.

"Poor girl," Aunt Louisa quipped.

"We ran into each other this morning, and she invited me. Quite impromptu."

Aunt Louisa grumbled. "Don't say I didn't warn you."

"I'm sure I won't get eaten alive."

Her aunt stared at her as if she had doubts.

"Can I come?" Gloria repeated.

"I think it would be poor form if I brought someone along," Rosa said diplomatically, "at least at this point."

Gloria pouted then took a sip of lemonade. "At least show me your new car."

"Of course," Rosa said. "Let's go."

THAT EVENING, Rosa drove her Corvette Roadster through the open wrought-iron gate and down the driveway of the Gainer Estate. The palm-tree-lined drive took her past manicured lawns and tennis courts and ended in a roundabout that circled an impressive five-tiered concrete fountain. The residence itself was a two-story Mediterranean Revival-style home that appeared to be even bigger than the Forrester mansion. Rosa pulled up to the steps leading to the front entrance, and a chauffeur immediately appeared and took her keys. He gave her a ticket stub to reclaim her car, and she watched, rather nervously, as he pulled away from the curb and disappeared around the side of the house.

Inside, the lobby ceiling arched heavenward, echoing with the clip-clopping of high-heel shoes as Janet Gainer walked briskly toward her.

"Thanks so much for coming, Miss Reed." She shook Rosa's hand.

Rosa returned, "It's good to see you again, Mrs. Gainer. And you must call me Rosa."

"Of course," Janet said, her cheeks blushing at her faux pas. The charade they were about to engage in required that they be old friends. "And you must call me Janet."

Janet led Rosa to the back of the house, through a wide, arched-ceiling breezeway and into a massive terraced backyard that featured three swimming pools, one on each terraced level. The top two pools cascaded water into the lower, larger pool, which also had a tile fountain at the center of it. Rosa was glad she'd worn her best party dress.

Spotlights lit a manicured lawn that had palm trees and Roman-style facades that gave the entire back garden a surreal Romanesque ambiance. Rosa felt like she was taking a stroll through the garden of some ancient Roman emperor; all that was missing were the togas and tunics. Contradicting this illusion was a man playing soft jazz on a grand piano parked on the corner of the terrace.

The gathering of about thirty people—a mix of men in designer suits and women in high-fashion dresses—paused their conversations when they spotted her with Janet Gainer.

Since they seemed to have everyone's attention, Janet spoke to the group. "Everyone, this is Rosa. She's the niece of a dear friend of mine from London."

A young man with sandy-blond hair oiled back with a duckbill curl over his forehead approached. He held a drink in one hand and pinched a lit cigarette with the fingers of the other. He appraised Rosa appreciatively.

"Colin," Janet began. "I would like you to meet Rosa Reed, visiting from London. She's the niece of a friend of mine. Rosa, this is Colin Monahan."

As he shook her hand, the man intently looked at her. His eyebrows furrowed slightly. "Hey, I think there was a gal named Rosa Reed from London that went to high school here," he said. "Was that you?"

Now that Rosa saw him close, the fellow did look rather familiar.

"Yes, I did go to school here for a time. Santa Bonita High."

He grinned crookedly. "I remember you. The only girl in the whole school with an accent."

Rosa had mentioned to Janet Gainer that she had lived in Santa Bonita as a teenager just in case this exact situation occurred. There was a good chance that anyone approximately Rosa's age would recognize her if they had gone to the same high school.

"It turns out that Janet and my aunt in London are acquainted," explained Rosa.

Colin Monahan's eyebrows rose in question.

"It was quite serendipitous that your Aunt Janet recognized me from a photograph my aunt sent in the mail," Rosa said. The story was fabricated but plausible.

"How could I mistake this face," Janet added, motioning to Rosa with flair.

Colin Monahan didn't take his eyes off Rosa. She couldn't tell if it was mere curiosity or something else.

"What have you been doing since eleventh grade, Mr. Monahan? Did you marry?" Rosa asked with a warm smile. She wanted to start him talking.

"Oh, well. That would be a long story, but in a nutshell, I ended up in imports and exports; and no, I have not found Miss Right just yet, though I am sure she's around somewhere." His eyebrow jumped in jest.

Rosa chuckled, "I am sure she is. So, what does that mean, importing and exporting?"

"Oh, I don't think you'll find it that interesting," Colin Monahan said, dismissively.

Rosa ignored the slight. "Of course I would. Come on, spill the beans."

Just then, a waiter came by with a tray of champagne. Rosa took a glass and raised it to her lips while keeping eye contact with Colin Monahan. She didn't want to be flirtatious, but her purpose here was to get information, so if it meant a bit of friendly banter, she was fine with that.

"Well," Colin started, "for example, last year I set up a special international investment corporation and invited investors to participate in buying bulk goods from Asia and selling them to large American retailers like Sears and Roebuck, Macy's, and Kmart stores."

"What kind of goods?" Rosa asked. She thought she saw a flash of guardedness come into his eyes.

"Oh, anything from shoes to hardware items. Boring stuff like that."

"I've had some limited experience in the international retail *and* import business," Rosa said, referring to her mother's Regent Street boutique dress shop, *Feathers & Flair*. But it was just a half-truth. She didn't know that much about international bulk import, but she brought it up to continue probing without being obvious.

"Really?"

"Yes. I had an unfortunate experience, however, getting involved with *family* on some of the larger ventures. That turned out to be a bad idea."

"I couldn't agree more." Mr. Monahan shook his head ruefully then glanced about while taking a sip of champagne. "Well, if you ladies will excuse me." He smiled and then nodded slightly to Rosa and Janet.

"Enjoy the evening." He walked away and back into the house, appearing rather in a hurry to disappear.

"I believe you hit a nerve there," Janet said under her breath. "Oh, there's Mr. Gainer."

Janet linked Rosa by the arm and approached a gentleman with a full head of white hair, bushy white eyebrows over stern blue eyes, and a deeply lined face marking a perpetual scowl. Though stooped over slightly, Mr. Orville Gainer had an air of authority that demanded respect, or at least, obedience. Rosa couldn't help but feel a slight tremor of intimidation.

He eyed Rosa with suspicion. "Who's this?"

"This is Rosa Reed from London," Janet said boldly. "She's the niece of an old friend, and my friend now too."

His blue eyes bore into Janet. "What is she doing here?"

"Oh, Orville, don't be rude. I invited her." She flashed the man a girlish smile. "I wanted her to see how well I've done."

Orville Gainer turned to Rosa and extended a hand. "A friend of Janet's is a friend of mine. I hope you enjoy your time in Santa Bonita."

Rosa fought the sudden urge to curtsey. "Thank you, sir."

Thankfully, Janet led Rosa away, a little further out into the yard.

"He's frightful," Rosa said.

Janet huffed. "I wish I could say he's all bark and no bite, but I'm pretty sure his bite is lethal."

Rosa hoped that was a metaphor.

They approached an attractive, fit-looking couple in their mid-fifties talking near the water fountain. The man looked like he was of Italian descent with black hair graying at the sides and brown eyes. After introducing Rosa and explaining the London connection, Janet said, "Rosa, this is Leo and Valerie Romano. Valerie is my husband's eldest sister." Janet had explained the relationships to Rosa earlier, but it was good to make a show of presenting the information as if for the first time. Rosa was pleased to be able to put faces to the names.

Leo Romano pointed his chin toward Colin Monahan who had rejoined the party. "I saw you talking to Colin."

"Yes, that's right," Rosa said. "He seems like a nice young man."

"Uh-huh," Leo took a sip of his drink with his eyebrows raised. "A *nice* young man is one way to describe him, perhaps. He needs a good wife to settle him down, though." He smiled at her. "You're single, aren't you?"

"Leo!" His wife jabbed him in the ribs with her elbow, almost causing him to spill his drink. She then looked apologetically at Rosa. "Please ignore my husband. He gets a little too forward sometimes after a drink or two."

"I suppose you're right," Leo Romano said and lowered his voice as he looked around the gathering. "I suppose this family has already had its share of rescue marriages."

His wife shook her head at him.

JUST THEN, a younger couple strolled by. The gentleman wore a crisp summer suit, cuffed at the ankles and had his blond hair trimmed short and oiled to the side in a sharp part. Handsome in an uptown way, his partner, a plump brunette and plain in appearance, paled next to him. Janet stopped the pair and then turned back to Rosa. "Rosa, meet my son, Sidney, and his fiancée, Debbie. Debbie is Leo and Valerie's daughter. And yes, they're cousins but didn't grow up together, so it's okay."

Rosa blinked at Janet's obvious discomfort and a failed attempt to smooth it over.

Sidney and Debbie extended a cool welcome.

A man in his fifties with a short, brown pompadour joined them and put his arm around Janet. In his other hand, he held a cigar. He reminded Rosa of the Scottish actor Sean Connery who had appeared regularly in a BBC police series called *Dixon of Dock Green,* which her parents loved to watch.

"Hello, everyone, so sorry I'm a bit late for the party. I hope Dad will forgive me. What do you think?" Before anyone could answer, he turned to Rosa. "Oh, hello."

"This is my friend Rosa Reed," Janet Gainer said. "Rosa, this is my husband, Michael." Earlier, Janet had told Rosa that her husband didn't know she'd called on a private detective. She scolded him playfully. "He believes in being fashionably late."

"How do you do?" Rosa offered her hand.

"I do alright, thanks." He smiled brightly and turned to Janet. "So, this is the niece of the old friend you told me about?"

"She is," Janet said. With a sly grin, she added, "I wanted her to see what kind of family I had married into, so she could report back to her aunt just how well I did."

Mr. Michael Gainer inclined his head. "Well, it's brave of you to come, Miss Reed. The Gainer family is a fruity bunch, all right. And I can say that because I was born into it. Those, like my poor wife, who've married into it had to learn the hard way." His chuckle held little mirth.

Michael guided Janet to the drinks table, and Janet waved for Rosa to follow. They interrupted a heated discussion in motion, and Rosa concluded that Dieter was the topic of interest.

"Well, who knows what he's up to?" A tall, bored-looking man said. "For all we know, he's gone chasing after aliens or God knows what." A woman beside him, standing so close that the two of them must have been a married couple, laughed as she lifted her drink.

"Remember last year when he thought that the government was hiding alien spaceships out in the desert? Crazy German! I bet that's where he is right now—somewhere in the Nevada desert with survival gear and binoculars."

Janet whispered in Rosa's direction. "Frank and Alice Monahan. Alice is the youngest sister."

A man who must have been Walter Gainer—he was a younger Orville Gainer from head to toe—joined in with a smirk. "Or when he insisted that the Russians were going to invade Washington DC?"

Leo Romano sipped his cocktail from a crystal glass. "I think Dieter was having flashbacks to the war when the Russians invaded Berlin!"

Rosa noted the disdain in Mr. Romano's voice.

"Well, let's not stand here and rag on Dieter," Michael Gainer said. "I am sure Miss Reed is not interested in hearing all this."

Rosa wondered if Michael Gainer was deftly trying to change the subject, perhaps uncomfortable with talking about Dieter Braun at length with a non-family member present.

"Wasn't there a project he had a few years back?" Leo Romano said. He seemed lost in thought and was obviously ignoring Michael. "Something about some doomsday scenario...yeah, that's it. I think he wanted to build a shelter. A *fallout shelter* he called it."

"Why is that so crazy?" Janet asked defensively. "Lots of people are concerned about a Russian atomic strike. In some schools, they teach children to 'duck and cover' and have drills to help them practice emergency procedures."

"I just don't believe that stuff," Leo Romano said dismissively. "If Khrushchev wanted to bomb us, he would have done it already. Besides, Dieter always takes things too far." He took a sip of his drink and then thought for a moment. "I do remember him saying that he hired a large truck to transport building materials to some remote destination near their cabin by Lake Fairbanks." He looked up at everyone as a new realization hit him. "I think he *did* build something crazy out there somewhere. I bet that's where he is!"

4

Could Dieter Braun be working on a bomb shelter? Was it possible he'd somehow got trapped in it? Was perhaps even now pounding on a locked door with the air supply running out? The thought produced a sudden surge of urgency to Rosa's quest to find the shelter.

Before leaving the party the night before, Rosa and Janet had agreed to an early-morning trip to Dieter Braun's cabin. Rosa's Corvette wasn't the right vehicle for the rough roads, so Janet had offered to take them in her Willy's Jeep and drove to the front entrance of the Forrester mansion shortly after breakfast.

Janet waved to Rosa through her open window.

"Hi, Janet," Rosa said as she opened the passenger door. "You don't mind if I bring my cat?"

Rosa had grown accustomed to the strange looks shot her way when she brought Diego along. "He thinks he's a dog. He even comes when I whistle." *Sometimes. When the whistle sounds like pssst.*

"I don't mind if he doesn't mind," Janet said. "It is a Jeep, so the drive will be bumpy, and there could be predators."

Rosa felt a stab of concern. "Predators?"

"Coyotes. Raccoons. That sort of thing."

The only wild creatures Rosa ever had to think about in England were foxes and deer, and neither posed much of a threat to cats.

Janet smirked at her hesitation. "He'll be fine. Get in."

"I'll be sure to keep him in my satchel." Rosa had chosen a brown one with small blue polka dots for this outing.

It was an hour and a half drive due east from Santa Bonita; an hour was on the paved highway after which, at a little town called Caldwell, Janet turned onto a dirt road. They chatted about England—No, Rosa hadn't met the new queen, and no, she couldn't imagine being thrust into such a role at such a young age—and California—did one tire of the constant good weather? They listened to the top forty on the radio, which lost reception as they got further into the wild.

As the Jeep slowly gained altitude on the winding road up to the glacier-fed Lake Fairbanks, Rosa took the time to question Janet about bits of conversations she had overheard at the party the night before.

"What did Mr. Romano mean when he mentioned 'rescue' marriages?"

Janet shifted into a lower gear as they climbed around another switchback. The ponderosa pine forest got thicker, and the air slightly cooler with each passing mile. "He was probably referring to Walter and Patricia." She hesitated for a long moment, obviously reticent to talk about it.

Rosa waited, letting the silence draw out, and was rewarded.

"When Walter Gainer met Patricia, she was an alcoholic. In fact, she had just divorced her first husband and was having a bad go of it. From all accounts, the alcohol had much to do with the divorce, though I don't know the details." Janet rubbed her forehead as if she could erase the lines that had formed there. "Anyways, she didn't have any children with her first husband either; that marriage didn't last very long. She managed to hide her heavy drinking, and Walter and Patricia were married less than a year later. Patricia was almost penniless at the time, and of course, Walter came from significant money.

"The whole Gainer family vehemently opposed the marriage, and even after they were married, there was a lot of criticism leveled at Walter for marrying a 'gold-digging lush' as Orville Gainer called her."

"How awful!" Rosa said sincerely. The saga of this family seemed to get darker and darker as the conversation progressed.

"Over the years, there have been lapses of alcohol abuse followed by stints with Alcoholics Anonymous. She's been sober now for almost sixteen years, but the stigma continues in the Gainer clan. She married Walter for his money, and he is too naive to realize it, at least that's what the perception is. However, I can tell you firsthand that their marriage appears solid. They have their moments, like any married couple. But from what I can tell, they are devoted to each other."

Eventually, the road led them to a small lake. Along the way, they had passed several properties with cabins nestled in the forest. But as they continued around the edge of the lake, Rosa noticed there were no more access roads or properties. They continued until Janet veered to the right and followed an even rougher road, which turned out to be a driveway to a small but nicely kept log cabin. Situated close to the quiet, sun-dappled lake, the dwelling had a dock that extended into the water. A rowboat was tied to one of the pillars. The scene was so idyllic that Rosa pictured herself reading a book with Diego on her lap, and curled up in front of a fireplace.

The tall ponderosa pines stood like silent sentinels shading the cabin, allowing just occasional shafts of sunlight to break through. Only the wide porch had the sun shining directly on it.

They climbed out of Janet's Jeep—both had chosen sensible outfits of Capri pants and sneakers. Rosa carefully took Diego out of her satchel and placed him on the grassy ground. She watched him closely in case he decided to scamper off, but he just sniffed the surrounding ground. He looked a bit frightened.

"It's a great big world out here, isn't it, little fella?" Janet said.

Rosa stood for a moment and listened. It was the quietest place she had ever experienced. The absolute absence of man-made sounds overwhelmed her. Inhaling deeply, she let the pine-scented air fill her lungs and clear her head. She removed her Argus 35mm camera from its case and a notepad from her satchel, and then picked up Diego to put him back inside. He seemed eager to climb in again.

Janet knocked on the cabin door. "Dieter?" She knocked louder the second time and shouted the man's name.

When there was no sign of him nor anyone else,

Rosa said, "Do you think he might be inside? Perhaps he's in trouble. He might need our help."

Janet frowned. "I'm afraid I don't have a key."

Rosa thought that quite unfortunate and decided to check under each porch step and on top of the window and door sills, but could find no spare key. She was about to pick the lock with a hairpin but noticed a planter at the far end of the porch. Underneath the pot, she found a key. If fit easily into the lock, and Rosa pushed open the front door.

"Voilà!"

JANET STARED at the key in consternation. "Now, why didn't I think of that?"

Rosa had a fleeting thought. *Good question. If Janet was as close to Dieter as she claimed, then why didn't she*?

Rosa followed Janet into the darkened cabin. When Janet clicked the switch by the wall phone, a light came on, and she muttered, "Good. There's light." She lifted the black phone receiver. "Dial tone."

The cabin was well kept. A wood stove for heat sat near the far wall. The sparse but serviceable kitchen led to a bathroom and a modest bedroom with a wooden closet and a single bed. The bed was made, the floor was swept, and the dishes had been left to dry in a wire rack.

Two wooden chairs were pulled up to a small table covered with a red-and-white linen cloth. On one of two padded lounge chairs, the book *Berlin Alexanderplatz* by Alfred Döblin lay open and facedown. Just beside the front door, a rack on the wall held two fishing rods and a Mauser M98 deer rifle with a scope. The gun was secured to the rack by a metal padlock.

But there was no sign of Dieter Braun.

With Diego strapped safely over her shoulder, Rosa searched the dry ground around the perimeter of the cabin for footprints but found none. Janet came out of the house, and the women walked to the end of the dock to the rowboat. It appeared to be freshly painted, a bright apple-red, and two wooden oars lay on the floor under the benches.

"Anything in the house?" Rosa said, scanning the area around the dock.

"Like someone woke up and cleaned the place today." Janet pointed at the rowboat. "A few months ago, Dieter said he needed to paint his boat. It looks like he did."

And his fallout shelter? An avid reader, Rosa knew about people's dread of Soviet invasion or fallout from nuclear bombs. Fallout shelters were a direct response to these fears. Such shelters were often built directly under the home, but Rosa guessed that the cabin was too close to the lake to dig deep. In that case, any shelter Dieter Braun might've built would be on higher ground, but to be quickly accessible, it would be close to the cabin.

Rosa set Diego back on the forest floor, and this time he immediately scampered off in the direction of a small opening in the thick forest growth. Rosa had to walk quickly to keep him in sight.

She grinned at Janet. "He must have already spied out a good toilet."

As they got closer, Diego stopped behind a small sapling, having made his choice of space to do his business. While he somewhat sheepishly tended to nature, Rosa looked around. Her gaze landed on a set of faint tire tracks. Once Diego had finished scratching his spot, she picked him up, placed him back in the satchel, and kept walking. Janet followed behind.

Neither spoke as they followed the tracks, which were obvious in the disturbed undergrowth. Soon tread marks came into view. On the other side of a small knoll, they found a dusty Land Rover. Next to it, an opened steel trapdoor on the ground.

They hurried to the opening.

"Dieter, are you there?" Janet called.

Peering inside the cemented cylindrical shaft, Rosa

could see nothing but a ladder propped up against one side.

"Dear God, what is that smell?" Janet pulled a handkerchief out of her purse and held it over her mouth and nose.

Rosa said nothing. As a former officer in the London Metropolitan Police, she recognized the fetid odor of a decomposing body. It took twenty-four to thirty-six hours before a corpse emitted gasses caused by bacteria consuming the body.

Rosa stared Janet in the eyes. "Let me go down. You can hold Diego for me."

Janet's mouth fell open, but she didn't protest. Silently, she took Rosa's satchel.

After tying a handkerchief over her nose, Rosa removed a flashlight and a pair of rubber gloves from her purse. After putting the gloves on, she turned on the flashlight and carefully descended. Reaching the bottom, she found herself in a rectangular-shaped room with three bunk beds, a kitchen table with chairs, electrical equipment, and two sets of metal shelving, one of which appeared to be bolted to the walls. The shelf contained tools—all with the initials DB scratched into them—water containers, and a large amount of packaged foods.

The other set of shelves had fallen over, and food was strewn across the floor. Pinned underneath, Rosa could see a man in blue overalls lying facedown. Congealed blood had puddled next to his head. She stepped over scattered tools and equipment that had fallen off the shelving unit and checked for a pulse. As she expected, there was none. Rosa checked her watch and wrote in her notebook.

5

"Is everything OK down there?" Janet shouted from on top of the entrance shaft.

Rosa peered up at her new friend. "It looks like there's been an accident." She softened her voice. "It's Dieter. I'm afraid he's deceased. I don't think you should come down."

"Oh no." Janet cupped her mouth with her hand. "You're sure?"

Rosa nodded. "Please call the police and an ambulance. Can you do that?"

Janet nodded then disappeared.

Judging from the state of decomposition, Rosa guessed that death had occurred approximately two to three days earlier. The wound—a bloody matting of his hair at the back of his head—was easy to see. Made from steel, the shelving unit was sturdy and heavy. One of the beams of the shelf was dented and was probably what had struck Mr. Braun on the head.

Rosa picked up a battery-operated searchlight she'd spotted lying on the floor and switched it on, flooding the room with its beam. She set it down on a table, prepared her camera, then snapped pictures of the wound, the body in full, and the surrounding area. Lying next to Mr. Braun's right hand was a chrome socket wrench. Rosa snapped a picture.

Mr. Braun might've been attempting to reinforce the shelving. Two bolts stuck out of the wall near the ceiling. Rosa searched the floor for the corresponding nuts and found them a few feet from the body. She examined them closely and took pictures.

Around the base of the ladder, Rosa noticed a small amount of fresh tobacco strewn on the landing. She took a picture then removed her gloves. Picking up a few strands, she crumbled it and sniffed.

When Rosa was finally satisfied that she had everything noted, measured, and photographed, she returned to the surface.

Back in the cabin, Rosa made Janet tea—Mr. Braun was well stocked—as they waited for the police to arrive. Janet wasn't the only one who needed her nerves soothed by the tea. Rosa was certain that Detective Miguel Belmonte would show up. Though they were in the boonies as they called it in America, the cabin and outlying areas fell in the Santa Bonita jurisdiction.

To complicate matters, she expected Dr. Larry Rayburn to arrive as well. Chief Medical Examiner Dr. Philpott wasn't likely to be interested in making the long drive to Lake Fairbanks, and his assistant was the only alternative.

Rosa and Larry had been on several dates over the past few weeks, and Rosa liked him.

But she loved Miguel, this she couldn't deny, even after all this time. Unfortunately, Miguel had moved on. A real barrier named Charlene Winters lay between them now.

Rosa released a long breath, determined to remain professional, no matter how hard it would be to ignore her emotions.

"Orville is going to be so upset with me," Janet said.

"Why? You are the reason your brother-in-law has been *found*."

"Because I called the police. Orville likes to deal with matters in-house, so to speak."

"But, surely, not when it comes to a death."

Janet raised a brow. "*Especially* when it comes to a

death." She gave Rosa a knowing look. The only people who didn't like to involve the police were people with something to hide.

The sound of gravel crunching announced somebody's arrival. Rosa's heart jumped. Miguel or Larry? She pulled on the curtain to peer outside.

Miguel.

"It's the police," Rosa said. "If you like, I can deal with them. At least, initially."

Relief flashed across Janet's face. "Would you mind? I'll keep your kitten company."

Rosa nodded, and after a fortifying breath, headed outside. Miguel and his partner, Detective Sanchez, along with Officer Richardson, the police photographer, had just exited the black-and-white police cruiser.

"Hello, Detective Sanchez, Detective Belmonte," Rosa said. She added an obligatory greeting to Officer Richardson, who seemed to have an issue with a "female consultant from London" getting involved in Santa Bonita Police work.

Miguel's gorgeous copper-brown eyes flickered at her use of his formal title.

"Hello, Miss Reed," he returned. "Fancy meeting you here."

"I was hired by Mrs. Janet Gainer," Rosa explained. "She was worried about a missing family member. My search led us here. It turns out that her brother-in-law took the current concerns about the global atomic threat to heart and built a bomb shelter." Rosa pointed. "It's behind the cabin."

"I see," Miguel said. "Please lead the way."

"What about the medical examiner?" Rosa asked.

"He'll find us." Rosa thought that was likely, especially since Janet was in the cabin and could point the way.

She stepped in front of the men and started toward the shelter. Despite her vow to remain professional, she couldn't help but think about how she looked from the back. Was her hair mussed from the handkerchief she'd worn? How did her capri pants look—were the fellows watching her behind?!

To rein in her thoughts, she asked awkwardly, "How are things down at the precinct?"

"Oh, you know. Sanchez and I keep things under control."

Rosa could hear the mirth in Miguel's voice as he continued.

"He eats a lot of pastry, and I scold him. It's a tension-filled relationship, but we make it work."

Rosa couldn't see Detective Sanchez, who took the rear, but heard him grunt.

They came into the clearing, which allowed

Miguel to step in beside her. "I understand you were the one to find the body?"

"I was."

"Does this stuff follow you around?"

Miguel referred to a previous case at the beginning of summer when Rosa happened upon a dead carnie at the boardwalk fair.

"It's a gift, I guess."

"Some gift."

At the entrance of the bunker, Rosa said, "The body's down there. I recommend covering your noses."

Miguel went down first, followed by Detective Sanchez and Officer Richardson, the latter casting a disparaging look her way. He was the reason she'd taken her own photographs. There was no way Officer Richardson would share his with her.

Rosa debated whether she should join the police, but the space was rather cramped, and she didn't want to get in the way. As it was, she heard footsteps coming from the path, and she couldn't help but break into a smile when Larry came into view, black medical bag in hand.

"Hello, darlin'," he said with his endearing Texan drawl. His smile matched hers. "How'ya doin'?"

Physically, Larry Rayburn was a negative image of Miguel with his blond hair and blue eyes, but the men shared the same sense of duty and competency where their jobs were concerned. And both were charming and endearing in their own way.

Larry kissed her on the cheek, and Rosa couldn't help but cast a glance toward the bunker entrance, relieved that Miguel hadn't seen it. Though she and Larry had been dating, they hadn't come to an understanding yet.

"The boys are already here, I see," Larry said.

"Yes, Detectives Belmonte and Sanchez and Officer Richardson are below. It's a rather small space."

"I suppose they'll have to make room for me," Larry said as he started down the ladder. He was a tall man, and Rosa was certain one of the officers would soon surface to make space. She was correct; Detective Sanchez's hat soon popped from the hole and eventually his entire rumpled self made it out safely.

"What do you make of it?" Rosa asked.

Detective Sanchez held his forearm to his nose as if that would help get rid of the smell that came with him from below. "Looks like the guy took a tumble while trying to secure the shelving to the wall."

Rosa hummed. That had been her conclusion on first look too. She'd wait to see what Larry and Miguel thought.

Eventually, the ambulance arrived, and the body was removed from the bunker.

Rosa stared at Miguel. "What do you think?"

"Probably accidental death, but I'll wait until the autopsy is completed before calling it."

"I'll get on that first thing in the morning, Detective," Larry said. He turned back to the shelter. "That's quite somethin', isn't it? The fellow really believed the Russians are gunna send over one of those nuclear bombs."

"To be fair, the arms race *is* intense," Miguel said. "They're crashing rockets in the desert, left and right, trying to beat the Russians into space."

Larry nodded somberly. "God help us if they succeed."

Standing rather awkwardly in a small circle, Rosa, Miguel, and Larry were the last ones at the scene. Larry finally motioned to the path. "Should we go?"

"I'd like a moment with Miss Reed, Dr. Rayburn," Miguel said, "if you don't mind."

Larry blinked, looking stumped. "Why sure, um—" To Rosa's horror, he leaned down to kiss her again, she turned her head sharply to make sure his lips landed on her cheek.

Larry smiled at her, seemingly oblivious to her sudden mortification. "See you tonight, *Miss Reed*."

As Rosa watched Larry go, she could feel Miguel's eyes boring into the back of her head. When she turned, his gaze locked on her with a look of disbelief. "Are you and Larry Rayburn dating?"

Rosa folded her arms against her chest. "We've gone on a few dates, not that it's any of your business."

"Yes, you're right. I apologize. Please, let's forget I said anything." Miguel cleared his throat then waved toward the bunker. "What were your thoughts about this?"

"I'm not convinced it was an accident."

Miguel's eyes rose to meet hers again. "Oh? Why not?"

"I'm not prepared to say right now. Like you, I want to wait to find out what Larry, er, Dr. Rayburn discovers."

Miguel sighed. "Very well."

"Was that what you wanted to say to me?" Rosa asked. Hardly a reason to create a forced farewell with Larry when the three could've walked together to the parked vehicles.

"Actually, there is something else. Since you've been hired by one of the Gainers, I thought I should let you know that the Gainer family has been under investigation several times over the years."

Based on what Janet had hinted at, Rosa wasn't surprised.

"Nothing has ever been proven," he added. "Sanchez and I are investigating another case right now involving the Gainer family."

"What kind of investigation?" Rosa asked

"You know that I am not at liberty to give any details."

"All right."

"However, I can tell you that all the investigations have centered around fraud: insurance fraud, real estate, embezzlement, and the like. That family has woven a tangled web over the years.

They returned to the cabin and, after a stiff goodbye, parted ways. Rosa went inside to join Janet Gainer, whose eyes were filled with dread.

"I think I should tell the family who you are," she said.

"Why's that?" Rosa asked.

"They're going to find out anyway, and I want to stay a step ahead. I'm calling a meeting for this evening. Can you come?"

"Of course." Rosa found Janet's robotic demeanor unnerving. "Janet, are you all right? You've had quite a shock."

"I don't think it was an accident," Janet said. "I think Dieter was murdered."

After a moment, Rosa nodded. "I think you're right."

6

Rosa spent the rest of the afternoon in her office darkroom, developing the pictures. She picked up Chinese food from a restaurant down the street and sat at her desk to review her notes while she ate. She didn't yet have any cat food at the office, but she did have some milk. Although Diego also enjoyed a taste of chicken chow mein.

Once the photographs were developed and dry, Rosa stopped at the Forrester mansion to drop off Diego with her cousin Gloria, who was happy to take care of him for a few hours. She then changed into a navy streamline pencil dress with wide hip pockets and buttons that ran from the collar to the hem. With a pair of white kitten heel shoes—a nearly flat slip-on with thimble-like heel—a pearl collar necklace, and a blue, feather-trimmed fascinator hat pinned to the side, Rosa felt professional and stylish. Two attributes she needed to face the formidable Gainer clan, who were quite likely going to see her with a collective disregard. It helped that Rosa drove her new Corvette onto the estate. She was savvy, educated, and experienced at police work. She would *not* be intimidated.

As before, a butler parked her Corvette, and Janet, who'd also swapped her dusty capris for a fashionable dress, met her at the door.

"Most of them are here. They don't yet know why I called the meeting, but one thing they can't bear is to miss out on perceived gossip and scandalous news. They know about Dieter's death and likely presume I'm going to make an emotional fool of myself."

Janet led Rosa through the large open foyer and into the living room where the Gainer family was assembled.

The tastefully decorated Spanish-tiled room had several large leather couches and wingback chairs along with finely upholstered lounge seats. The family members sat in a circle around a large glass coffee table.

Orville Gainer occupied one of the button-back armchairs; his expression was of a man who didn't like his time wasted. Sitting on one of the leather couches, Leo and Valerie Romano looked unsettled. Janet's husband, Michael, sat next to Colin Monahan on the couch. Colin's mother, Alice Monahan sat upright in the other armchair; her legs crossed at the ankles, her husband Frank standing behind.

Walter and Patricia Gainer, along with Sidney Gainer and his fiancée, Debbie Romano, were also present.

When Michael Gainer saw Janet and Rosa walk into the room, he approached them. "Everyone is waiting for someone to take charge of the meeting."

In a loud, raspy voice, Orville Gainer proclaimed. "For God's sake, Janet. What is this all about? We already know about Dieter's unfortunate demise. You're not going to get weepy on us, are you? And why on earth did you bring your 'friend' again?"

"I'll be as clear and quick as possible, Dad," Janet said. She accepted a drink Michael had brought her, took a sip, then started, "I want to thank you all for coming."

Sidney sniffed. "Get on with it, Mom. Debbie and I have plans."

"Patience, Sidney." Janet was trying to sound authoritative, but her voice held a bit of quaver. "Today has been a very emotional day for me, and I am still reeling from all of this. There are things you are not aware of regarding Dieter's death. First, I need to reintroduce Miss Rosa Reed. Most of you met her at our gathering last night, but what none of you know is that she is a private detective."

A murmur erupted.

Orville Gainer's blue eyes turned ice cold. "What kind of game are you playing, Janet?"

Janet held up a palm. "Please, hear me out. Miss Reed has served for many years as a distinguished member of the London Metropolitan Police."

"We are naturally impressed with the young lady's accomplishments," Leo Romano said, "but what does she have to do with us?"

A wave of discontent threatened to drown out Janet's voice and end the meeting before it began. Rosa stood and clapped her hands.

"Please, everyone. Let me explain."

The Gainers had enough social graces to quiet down, and Rosa was certain they were curious about her. Colin Monahan's eyes flashed with amusement.

"Janet came to me yesterday out of concern for her brother-in-law," Rosa started. "Apparently, *none* of you thought to go looking for him." Her gaze swept accusingly across everyone in the room. At this moment, she was glad for her London accent. It made her sound more like a schoolmarm scolding a classroom. "It's a jolly good thing Janet decided to act. Otherwise, Mr. Braun's body would *still* be rotting in the forest. Who knows how long it would have been before he was found?" The room grew deathly quiet.

Orville Gainer looked thunderstruck—his mouth half-open in a speechless mask. His gnarly knuckles grew white from gripping the arms of his chair.

Through tight lips, he said, "Get on with it or get out."

"Yes, I will, on both counts. I want to respect this family's privacy," she pronounced it *prih-vah-cee,* "and I don't want to stick my nose where it shouldn't be, but I highly suspect you have a bigger problem on your hands than you think. I'll explain, and then you can decide how to handle the landslide of unwanted attention that will soon befall this family."

"What do you mean 'unwanted attention'?" Frank Monahan asked.

"Yes, and what do you mean by 'bigger problem'?" Alice Monahan added.

"It is my professional opinion that Dieter Braun was murdered," Rosa said, "and I believe that the autopsy will confirm this."

The room became instantly electric. Everyone was either speechless with mouth hanging agape, or giving an exclamation of outrage or incredulity.

"This is ridiculous," Walter finally said. He beseeched Orville Gainer. "Dad?"

All eyes zeroed in on the elderly man, Rosa's included. *Would he shut her down, or let her continue?*

It was as if everyone held his or her breath, waiting for Orville Gainer's pronouncement. Then, the corner of his lip twitched. "We might as well hear the fairy tale she's concocted."

For a moment, nothing was said, then Valerie Romano finally broke the silence. Her voice was quiet but firm. "If someone killed Dieter, I damn well want to know about it." She scanned everyone's face. "Especially if it was one of you!"

"Now Val . . ." Leo Romano cut off his wife and patted her firmly on the back. To Rosa, he said, "Please, Miss Reed. Tell us what you know."

With one last glance around the room, Rosa picked up a leather briefcase she'd borrowed from Clarence and removed her notepad and a cream-colored file folder which contained copies of the photos she'd taken at the scene.

"First, I have a question," she said with her pen poised over a clean page. "Am I correct in surmising that Mr. Braun rolled his own cigarettes?"

Alice flicked a hand, fingers heavy with jeweled rings. "Yes."

"Does anyone know what brand of tobacco he used?" Since Alice had answered the question, Rosa stared at her for the answer, but the lady tightened her lips, apparently not wanting to cooperate any longer.

"Viceroy." Patricia Gainer said. "I rolled them for him on occasion."

Her husband, Walter, shot her a look of surprise.

"*What*?" Patricia Gainer responded. "He gave me a few in return. I can't drink, but at least I can smoke occasionally."

"Which pocket did he usually carry the tobacco pouch in?" Rosa asked.

Mrs. Patricia Gainer could hardly keep the contempt from her voice as she addressed Rosa. "His shirt pocket or in his overalls breast pocket."

"Very good," Rosa said. "Thank you. Now I must warn you some of these photographs are graphic." She leaned down, removed the first photograph, and flipped it over. It showed a picture of the fallen shelf with Dieter Braun's body pinned underneath, the congealed blood from the head wound visible on the floor. There were several gasps from around the room. Janet cupped her mouth with her hand.

Rosa continued, "At first glance, it looks like this heavy metal shelf fell on top of Mr. Braun and struck him on the head. I have no doubt there may also be several broken ribs. Perhaps a broken neck as well. As you can see in the photo, the shelf once contained several substantial items including a gas-powered air compressor, a box full of tools, and a small gas-powered generator."

With the tip of her pen, Rosa pointed to the items on the floor just beyond the body. Flipping the second picture, she highlighted the upended toolbox with tools scattered everywhere and the compressor lying on its side about five feet from the body.

"The trajectory indicates that they were placed on either the middle shelf or near the top. The same for the generator, which landed a few feet further. This would make the shelf very top-heavy."

Rosa flipped over the next picture. "You can see the two bolts cemented into the wall and extending out by about two and a half inches. Each of the six shelves has these same bolts. The difference is that the other shelves are all fastened with chrome nuts and flat washers to prevent them from falling. The shelf that fell on Mr. Braun didn't have any nuts attached. You'll see from the first photograph that he has a socket wrench in his hand. I found two chrome nuts not far from the body along with two flat washers."

Orville Gainer growled in Janet's direction. "I don't see what we need this woman for. There was an earthquake a few days ago, and Dieter was caught in the moment of bolting the shelf to the wall when it hit. It very obviously crashed on top of him." He spread his hands wide and shrugged his shoulders. "The socket wrench is in his hands; the nuts are lying close by on the floor. Case closed."

Rosa exhaled through her nose, reining in her impulse to put Mr. Gainer in his place. If he'd enrolled in detective studies in the Metropolitan Police Training School, he'd have just failed. Jumping to conclusions was the first thing they taught you *not* to do.

Rosa forced a smile. "It's not as simple as that, I'm afraid."

She leaned forward and flipped over the next photo. "This is a photo of the bottom shelf." With her pen, she pointed to a faint square outline on the shelf surface. "Toolboxes usually get oily from the tools inside if they are not always cleaned properly. Even the toolbox belonging to a most fastidious mechanic will have a bit of dust mixed with grime on it. The outside of the toolbox that we saw upended on the floor next to the body was slightly grubby. This faint square outline you see here is a bit of grime. It forms the exact measurement of the bottom of the toolbox."

Rosa looked up at everyone. "This indicates that originally, the toolbox was placed on the lowest shelf, not on a higher shelf as its trajectory suggests. No one with any kind of mechanical sense places heavy objects on a high shelf, especially in an area that may be prone to earthquakes. The same is true for the compressor."

Rosa pointed to four small, round grime marks on the lower shelf. "These correspond exactly to the rubberized legs of the air compressor. By the way, I found several pneumatic tools in a closed cabinet, the kind powered by compressed air, which explains why Mr. Braun kept an air compressor in the shelter."

"What exactly are you saying?" Walter Gainer asked.

Rosa glanced at each person in the room before answering. "I believe the scene was staged."

Rosa flipped over the next picture. "Here's a picture of the interior of the cabin. Does anyone notice anything strange?"

Everyone looked at the picture but said nothing.

"If we are to believe that the earthquake caused Dieter Braun to lose his balance and that the shelf subsequently fell as a result, why aren't things out of place in the cabin?" Rosa looked up at everyone's blank face. "Not one item spilled onto the floor from the shelves. I would guess that the effects of the earthquake along the coast were hardly noticeable in the area of Lake Fairbanks. I'm willing to bet that the weather bureau that records seismic activity will confirm this." She looked around the room. "Furthermore, I am not a pathologist, but I can assure you that Dr. Rayburn will rule that the gap between the time of death and discovery of the body will be at the most three days, perhaps four. It's been two days since the tremor. I believe the killer was betting on the complacency of this family, because the more time that passed, the harder it would be to determine when Dieter Braun died."

There was silence in the room.

"Shall I go on?" Rosa asked. She glanced at Janet, who looked sickly pale, and Rosa wondered if she now wished she hadn't asked Rosa to stay involved. "I have more pictures."

With a faint voice, Janet said, "Please do."

Rosa consulted her notes and then flipped over another photograph. "This is a close-up of the head wound—probably the blow that killed him. Again, I'll have to confirm this with Dr. Rayburn after the autopsy. At first glance, it looks like the rail from the shelf hit him, however, on closer examination of the wound, you can see two divots in the scalp that go quite deep."

"Yes, I see that," Patricia Gainer said. She looked like she was growing more and more intrigued by Rosa's detective work. "What does that mean?"

"It means that a flat rail from a falling shelf did not make that wound." The stunned family stared at Rosa, who stared right back. *If the killer were in this room, he—and I'm now convinced it is a 'he'—would probably get nervous about now.* "In fact, it looks to me like the claw end of a framing hammer made these marks.

"A framing hammer?" Janet's voice was almost a whisper.

"The kind of hammer a builder uses to build the frame of a house."

As if they were one organism, the Gainer clan shifted nervously, everyone focusing on each other with new suspicion.

"I'm assuming Dieter Braun owned such a hammer," Rosa continued. "Hammers are a natural part of any basic tool collection."

"Did you find a hammer?" Michael Gainer asked.

"I did not, and I'm assuming the police will be looking for it when my suspicions are confirmed by the autopsy. Detective Belmonte, who will no doubt lead the investigation, is a crack of a detective."

"If Uncle Dieter was killed by a strike to the head with a hammer," Colin Monahan said, "why is he under that shelf?"

"It's possible that Mr. Braun and the man who killed him had an argument that ended with a crime of passion involving the hammer," Rosa said. "Then, the killer tried to make it look like an accident caused by the recent earthquake. I also think the murder did not happen in the bomb shelter."

Janet Gainer had hired Rosa to find Dieter Braun

with an added request to explain to the Gainer family what had happened to him. Rosa had learned more about the case but felt it prudent to keep some information close to her chest for now.

Sidney Gainer stepped up to look closely at the photographs. "Well, I'll be damned."

7

Although Larry had offered to escort Rosa from the Forrester mansion to dinner, Rosa insisted it would be more expedient if she drove directly from the Gainer estate.

Feeling satisfied with her performance, and particularly being one up on old Mr. Gainer, demonstrated by the perturbed look on his usually smug face, Rosa sang along to "Shake, Rattle & Roll", while replaying the evening in her mind. She'd gotten her first client and had completed her assignment in good time. Working as a private investigator suited her just fine.

Rosa checked her wristwatch after parking in the lot behind the restaurant. *Exactly on time.* Larry had made reservations at a restaurant called *The Best Beach,* which had a beachfront location. Unlike the cooler, moodier beaches common in

England, California beaches were miles of white sand, lined with palm trees, and drenched with glorious golden sunshine or at this time of day, a dramatic sunset.

A smooth jazz trio played softly in the corner of the patio, and Rosa acknowledged the musicians with a smile. Her kitten heels click-clacked lightly across the cedar-wood patio to where Larry sat.

As soon as he saw her, he stood and greeted her with a kiss on the cheek.

"How d'ya like it?" He gestured around him, first at the restaurant and then at the ocean.

"It's wonderful," Rosa said.

Larry pulled her chair away from the table.

"Thank you."

Larry had proved to be a gentleman from their first date.

"It's my upbringin'," he had explained. "We Texans ain't nothin' if not polite."

Larry handed Rosa a menu. "Everythin' is delicious. This place reminds me of my favorite restaurant in Galveston. Overlooks the Gulf of Mexico." He grinned, and Rosa couldn't help but admire his southern charm. "I like to come here when I'm feelin' a bit homesick."

Rosa commiserated. "I understand homesickness. Such an interesting phenomenon when you think about it. The absence of a place creating a physical pain."

"So true." Larry closed his menu. "Homesickness can cause sleeplessness, lack of appetite, and headaches for some people," he said as if speaking to a patient.

"Do you get back to Galveston very often?" Rosa asked.

"Not as much as I'd like. California is great, but there's no place like home, is there?"

Rosa simply nodded. She missed London but wasn't ready to venture back there quite yet.

"Galveston isn't as far away as London," Larry continued, "and not a replacement, to be sure, but I'd love to take you there someday."

Rosa blinked at the surprising invitation. She was thankful the wine had arrived, and to avoid replying, she took a sip.

They both ordered steak dinners. After a few bites and comments on how delicious everything was, they settled into a comfortable conversation.

"Tell me more about your parents," Larry said. "I find it fascinating that they are *both* detectives?"

Rosa smiled. "It is a fun story, especially in light of my own chosen vocation. My father, Basil Reed, went through the ranks at Scotland Yard and retired as a superintendent. My mother, Ginger, ran a detective agency she called Lady Gold Investigations."

"Ginger? What a great name!"

Rosa laughed. "I agree. And no one suits a flamboyant name like that more than my mother. She's the type of person who commands a room the second she walks into it. She also ran her own successful boutique dress shop."

"Your childhood must've been very interestin'."

"Well, they didn't exactly tell me what they did from day to day when I was young, but after the war..." Rosa hesitated. She'd already told him that she'd lived with the Forrester family during that time, but she'd been purposefully vague in the telling. "After the war, my parents took me under their wings and mentored me in all aspects of their occupations."

"They must've seen your potential," Larry said.

Rosa was sure he was right, but she knew there was much more to it. After returning to London, Rosa had been emotionally broken, and her parents did what they could to help her heal—which for them meant keeping their daughter in sight and busy.

Larry asked, "How does London compare with Santa Bonita?"

"Well, London is damper, more crowded. The people are generally more formal and reserved, and the food is rather bland." She grinned at Larry. "But it also has beautiful architecture, a rich culture, and history in every cobblestone. I love it."

"Sounds fascinatin'."

"Even more important, we have cricket."

"We have crickets in Texas too."

Rosa burst out laughing. "Not the insect, the game."

Larry chuckled, and Rosa appreciated his ability to be a good sport about things.

"You mean that game that wishes it were American baseball."

Rosa smirked in return. "I do believe cricket has been around much longer than that adolescent game."

"Do you play?" Larry asked.

"No, not at all. I'll admit I find it boring. My father is a big enthusiast, though."

"I'm not sure I see the appeal." He shrugged his shoulders.

Rosa, eager to promote the intricacies of her home country, added with a note of triumph,

"We have a queen."

"Oh yeah, I heard y'all had a queen. What happened to the King?"

"Sadly, he passed away."

"So, the Queen is not married?" Larry looked incredulous.

"Oh yes, she's married to the Duke of Edinburgh."

"Edinburgh! Why even a good ol' boy like me from Galveston knows that Edinburgh is in Ireland, not in England."

Rosa's hand flew to her mouth to suppress a giggle. She didn't want him to think she was making fun of him. "Actually, it's in Scotland," she finally managed. She cut a piece off her steak.

"Aha, so he's Scottish."

"He was born in Greece." She lifted the piece of steak to her mouth.

"Greece? Well, how in the blue thunderin' heaven did a *Greek* man get to be a Duke of *Edinburgh* when he was born in a place where they've never even heard of bagpipes? I heard they dance on tables and play those bazooka guitars in Greece, for crying out loud."

"*Bouzouki*," Rosa corrected, waving her fork at him and grinning.

"Good golly, that guy must be luckier than a skinny turkey at Thanksgivin'."

Rosa's laughter filled her voice as she tried to explain. "His title when he was born was Prince Philip of Greece *and* Denmark."

Larry threw up his hands. "No wonder they didn't let him be king. He's already taken over most of Europe. Man, I have to meet this guy."

The twinkle in Larry's eyes told Rosa that he'd been pulling her leg about his lack of knowledge of the "old world", but she enjoyed hearing his down-home perspective of the royal family and the state of affairs in jolly old England. Rosa hadn't had a good laugh like this in a long time.

Larry Rayburn was charming in a disarming way. Rosa enjoyed hearing him describe, with love, his parents and his older sister and his affection for his home state of Texas. Rosa had never been there, but after tonight, she knew she wanted to visit there one day.

Larry seemed genuinely interested in everything about her. He'd hung on every word as she relayed her sojourn in America when only a child. He'd expressed astonishment at her position as a police officer in London, especially for a woman. Larry was truly impressed.

In turn, Rosa admired Larry's brave struggle out of a lower-class family and to becoming the top graduating student at a medical school in Los Angeles.

The time flew by, and before Rosa knew it, they were starting on a wonderful apple pie dessert, topped with a scoop of vanilla ice cream. Rosa had just popped the first delicious morsel into her mouth when she looked up and saw Miguel Belmonte walk onto the patio.

Her heart felt as if it had just headed downward on an out-of-control Ferris wheel.

Wearing a casual polo shirt and a pair of double-pleated trousers, Miguel looked like he'd come straight from a *LIFE* magazine shoot.

Miguel's fiancée, a stunning platinum blonde, had her arm hooked into his. Rosa instantly recognized the aspiring actress, Charlene Winters, and the speed and strength of her jealousy hit her hard. Her history with Miguel was still very much a part of her, it seemed, and she was greatly annoyed at that revelation. She was having a beautiful evening with a handsome and charming man, yet a glimpse of her teenage sweetheart with another woman had her mind swirling.

Larry, with his back to Miguel, was oblivious to Rosa's new turmoil. Her mind raced. She needed a plan to escape. The ladies' room was across the restaurant, and she couldn't get there without traipsing in full view of Miguel and Charlene.

She took a long sip of her wine, nearly finishing the glass.

Por todos los santos!

Rosa silently chastised herself. She needed to steady her emotions before either Larry or Miguel could read her mind.

It was fine. Everything was fine. She was on a date with Larry, which Miguel already knew about, and Miguel was with Charlene. She and the aspiring actress had briefly met before, and Rosa couldn't fault the lady's manners. *She was gracious and delightful and*, Rosa thought uncharitably, *not at all threatened by Rosa's presence in Miguel's life.*

The thought of meeting like this felt intolerably awkward. But then, why should it be uncomfortable? Rosa was on a date, and Miguel was with his betrothed. *What could be simpler and more natural*? And yet, the thought of them seeing each other and small talking made her palms dampen and her teeth clench.

Rosa watched out of the corner of her eye as Miguel and Miss Winters were led to a corner table, and for an instant, she thought she might get off scot-free. She would suggest to Larry it was time for them to leave, and if they kept their backs to the corner—

"Well, look at that," Larry proclaimed. "There's Detective Belmonte."

He waved at the couple, and Miguel, when he caught Larry's eye, waved back. Rosa was mortified. She felt her mouth form a fake smile as she finger-waved at Miguel, but she knew the rest of her face was not cooperating. Charlene Winters stared at Rosa with an expression that suggested that Rosa should make her exit.

Rosa thought the worst was over, and each couple could continue with their evening, but Miguel had to ruin it by rising from his seat and walking over. Rosa supposed it was natural, since Miguel and Larry often worked together, and were on friendly terms.

Miguel, holding his hat in his hands, said smoothly, "Good evening, Rosa. Larry. How was your dinner?"

"Terrific," Larry answered. "And good to see you. Twice in one day!"

"Yes, and Rosa as well. I take it you were able to wrap things up with your client?"

"I was hired to find a missing man," Rosa said, "which I did, and then to explain to the family what I think happened."

Miguel stared at her pointedly. "I'd be interested in knowing what you think happened."

"Actually, I plan to come to the precinct tomorrow morning. I don't have anything urgent." She looked at Larry. "And nothing of import until the autopsy report is complete. Besides, you and Detective Sanchez were at the same scene. I doubt that I found anything that you two did not."

"I'd still like to hear your opinion."

"Say," Larry said, changing the subject, "let's cease with work for the evening. Miguel, why don't you bring your date over here and share a drink with us? I don't think I've officially met her. Is she your fiancée?"

Rosa felt sweat bead on her brow. "If you'll excuse me," she said without looking either man in the eye, "I need to use the ladies'."

The heat of mortification burst in her chest as she pushed through the door of the ladies' restroom. Her departure had been noticeably abrupt and not at all ladylike. She could only imagine what Larry and Miguel must be thinking.

Taking deep breaths, Rosa eyed her reflection in the mirror and pouted at the round red blotches that had formed on her cheeks. Using a handkerchief dampened with cold water, she patted her face, talking herself down as she did. Miguel and Larry were too involved in their conversation to notice how it had affected her. They were both too focused on Charlene Winters sitting gracefully, her dramatic beauty on display, to notice Rosa's discomfiture at Larry's impromptu invitation. She just had to pull herself together and return to her table as if nothing out of the ordinary had happened, as if she hadn't just gotten run over by an emotional dump truck. She would put her shoulders back and face Miguel and Charlene like it didn't matter to her one iota, not even if Miguel put an arm around Charlene or showered any affection on her.

Rosa was suddenly short of breath. She couldn't do it. She just simply couldn't.

The horror didn't end there. The door of the ladies' pushed open and who should walk in but Miss Winters herself.

"Oh, hello," Miss Winters said, looking confident and tremendously fashionable in her black-and-white striped swing dress. A black hat sat at an angle on her perfectly styled hair; the attached veil covered her eyes, making her look mysterious and glamorous. She stared at Rosa through the reflection of the mirror. "I thought you'd left."

"No, just decided to freshen up." Rosa opened her purse and removed a lipstick. Her pale lips needed a touch-up, but Rosa also didn't want to dash out and give Miss Winters the impression that she was intimidated.

Even if she was a bit.

Miss Winters did the same, topping off her already luxuriously red lips. *Quite unnecessarily*, Rosa thought, which made her think that Miss Winters had known Rosa was in the restroom. Had she felt it necessary to warn Rosa off? Perhaps, underneath all that glam, she was feeling a mite intimidated herself.

Rosa faced her and forced a smile. "I know you are Detective Belmonte's fiancée, but we've never been formally introduced. I'm Rosa Reed."

"Charlene Winters," Miss Winters returned. "I've heard a lot about you. The famous lady detective from England."

"I wouldn't say famous," Rosa said, "but I've

worked with the Santa Bonita Police Department in the past as a consultant."

"Uh-huh."

"I hear you're an actress."

Miss Winters' eyes brightened. "I've just got cast in a movie that's going to be made here in Santa Bonita. Miguel and I will be able to see each other more often." She pushed out her lower lip. "It's been so difficult with me living in Los Angeles."

Rosa commiserated, "I imagine it would be. How did you and Miguel meet?"

"Oh, it's such a funny story. I was on vacation with my family, the beach here is so quaint, and my father's car was broken into. He summoned the police, and it was Miguel who attended us. I was immediately smitten with those dimples, you know? And Father was so grateful. Later, we bumped into each other at the Chug Away Diner." Charlene leaned in and lowered her voice as if they were conspirators. "In truth, I followed Miguel there and made him think it was accidental. He invited me to join him, and as they say, the rest is history."

Rosa blinked back at the pain gripping her heart. "How nice. And what will you do once you're married? Will you give up acting and move to Santa Bonita?"

Charlene chortled. "Oh no, honey. A movie star has to live in L.A. Miguel can transfer to the city."

Miguel had never mentioned a plan to move back to Los Angeles, but Rosa supposed he wasn't obligated to reveal his future intentions to her.

"My father thinks I'm going through a phase." Miss Winters pulled on the handle of the restroom door and stared at Rosa over her shoulder. "He's not happy that I'm marrying a cop, especially an immigrant. But he's mistaken." She smiled with a glint in her eye. "And I love proving my father wrong."

8

Rosa had a fitful sleep filled with blasted dreams of Miguel—he was always dressed in his army uniform, his dark hair short against his scalp, and inevitably the dream ended with them walking through the park saying a heart-wrenching goodbye. It always took her half a day to recover, and by the time Rosa got to her office in the morning, she was still emotionally drained.

Diego claimed his spot on one of the chairs in the stream of light coming through the window. He licked his paw and wiped his forehead, more times than Rosa thought necessary, then curled into a ball, his furry stomach exposed, and closed his eyes.

How lovely it must be to be a cat!

On her way to work that morning, Rosa had stopped at the bank and deposited the check from

Janet Gainer. She should be celebrating her first paycheck and supposed she was doing just that the night before until Miguel's arrival had ruined it.

She shook her head to free her thoughts of him.

What she needed was a new client to focus her attention on. Rosa glared at the telephone sitting silently on her desk and huffed. The phone wasn't about to ring with another job just because she stared at it.

Pushing away from her desk, she glanced at her kitten who, with his big green-blue eyes, watched her.

"It's awfully quiet, isn't it, Diego?"

He continued to stare without blinking, his expression quite clearly unconcerned with Rosa's unease.

"Perhaps I should buy a radio with my earnings. I think I'll go and do that at once. You'll be all right here for a little while." Diego had food, water, and a litter box and could sleep just as well in her office as in her satchel.

Rosa had just grabbed her purse when a knock sounded at the door. Before she could invite her caller in, the door sprang open. Rosa hoped she held in her shock at seeing Mr. Orville Gainer standing in the doorway.

"Mr. Gainer?"

Orville Gainer stepped into her office. "Miss Reed."

Rosa motioned to the chairs not occupied by a brown tabby cat now sprawled out on his back in a most undignified manner. "Please have a seat."

"I'll stand if you don't mind. I won't be long."

Rosa clasped her hands in front of her. "Very well. What can I do for you?"

Mr. Gainer steadied his piercing blue eyes on her. "Have you already gone to the police?"

Even though she'd told Miguel she'd come to the precinct that morning, she hadn't felt emotionally fortified enough to do it yet. Though now, she was curious about the burr in Mr. Gainer's side. It was something big enough to have him come to her office alone.

Before she could answer, Mr. Gainer plowed on. "You should know that the authorities will get no cooperation from anybody in my family. I will see to it that the police will find themselves stonewalled by everyone they interview. Each one will have a solid alibi. Each and every one will be accounted for. It will be an unassailable wall, stronger than Fort Knox. Let the police knock on our door, but no one will answer."

"You know there are laws against that kind of thing," Rosa said. "Concealment of evidence, lying to the police, obstruction of justice." She raised an eyebrow in question. "Are you sure you want those kinds of charges leveled against members of your family? And as I see it, you would be on the top of the list to be subpoenaed, Mr. Gainer."

"I am not afraid of the police, and I am willing to take that chance. Besides, I am confident they won't get very far."

What on earth was hiding under the rugs at the Gainer household?

"If that Mexican detective gets too close, he will suddenly find himself looking for employment." He cocked his head to one side and nodded knowingly.

A pit formed in Rosa's belly. "What exactly are you implying?"

"Let's just say that I have friends seated in high places in this town and this county. Detective Belmonte won't even know what hit him."

Rosa held her breath. *Mr. Gainer knew Miguel was on the case.*

Her caller narrowed his eyes in a way that made Rosa feel like she was being carefully studied by a cobra ready to attack. "I've done my homework on you, Miss Reed. I know that Mr. Belmonte once meant a great deal to you."

Rosa's mouth fell open. Heat exploded in her chest, burst up her neck and across her cheeks. How dare this man! How could he?

"I don't know what you're talking about."

"It turns out that certain letters meant for you were

returned to sender. However, the sender, Mr. Belmonte, or Private Belmonte, as he was known at that time, was no longer stationed in Santa Bonita." His lined lips turned up crookedly. "I'm good friends with the postmaster, you could say."

Mr. Gainer raised a wrinkled palm. His eyes softened, and suddenly, he was everybody's benign grandfather. "I feel that you and I have gotten off on the wrong foot, Miss Reed. Believe it or not, I do want Dieter's murder to be solved. I won't allow murderers to be counted among the Gainer clan; I just don't want the police involved."

Rosa finally found her voice. "I'm not sure how I can be of service."

"You impressed me last night, Miss Reed. It's not often that I'm impressed. I want to hire you to lead the investigation."

Rosa was about to refuse but then hesitated. If she didn't take the case and solve the murder, Miguel was sure to take it on. If he lost his job, it could cost him his career. He'd have to leave Santa Bonita...

"I'll need full cooperation from every family member," she finally said.

"Done."

"And you realize that if I find the killer, I have to share my evidence with the police. Only they can make an arrest and make a conviction stick."

"I understand," Mr. Gainer said. "But you only have to submit evidence that pertains to the murder. Any peripheral information would be kept in-house." He looked her straight in the eye. "If in your investigation, you find that the killer is not part of our family, I would invite you to leave the case, and let the police handle the investigation. That is as long as *they* don't think one of us did it, of course. In other words, if someone from outside our family killed Dieter, then I have very little concern about it, but if someone from within our family did it, I want to know who that is first, even before the police."

"I'm afraid that's not possible. You might make a way for the killer to escape justice." Rosa did not doubt that Orville Gainer was powerful enough to do so. "And I definitely can't condone vigilantism."

"Very well," Mr. Gainer said after a moment's pause. "But you can keep me updated as you go. Correct?"

"Yes, I can do that."

"I suppose that will have to do."

"I'll also need access to financial records from you and any businesses that are under your influence." Rosa held Mr. Gainer's gaze. *He hadn't reckoned on that,* she thought. "And I want immediate priority for interviews with anyone in the family. Is that clear?"

"As a bell."

Orville Gainer turned to leave, but paused. "Miss Reed, you might want to look into those crazy conspiracy theorists in town. Dieter spent more time with them than he did his own family. I wouldn't be surprised if one nut turned on another."

9

Rosa had a pretty good hunch that Orville Gainer's last suggestion was a rabbit trail. But he was her client now, and she'd be remiss if she didn't investigate the theory.

She parked her Corvette in front of the brown stucco one-story building that had the words *Santa Bonita Rotary Club* painted over the entrance. A sandwich board propped up on the sidewalk announced the *Survive and Thrive Club* meeting. A quick phone call had confirmed that the club met each Saturday at 1 p.m.

Inside, Rosa heard chatter coming from a room that had the door propped open into the hallway. On it was a poster of a cartoon turtle with the caption: *Remember what Bert the Turtle says ~ duck and cover.*

Approximately thirty middle-aged people, mostly men, mingled around a table set up with an assortment of snacks and soft drinks, and a large coffee urn. Rosa helped herself to coffee, then thumbed through a catalogue advertising bomb shelter supplies. Many of the items she'd spotted in Dieter's bunker were illustrated there: the generator, tools, a water purifying system, along with basic needs like stackable dishes and space-age blankets.

A white-haired man with an unfashionable beard stood up on the podium, signaling to the attendees to take a seat. Rosa quietly claimed an empty chair in the back row.

"Hello, everyone," the man said. "My name is John Raymond and I am the president of our little club here in Santa Bonita. I know that some of you drive in from nearby towns and from as far south as Ventura and as far north as Las Cruces and we hope you feel welcome in our beautiful town." His gazed landed on Rosa and flashed with interest. Rosa wondered how often new people attended these weekly meetings.

Mr. Raymond cleared his throat and went on. " Most of us here in the *Survive and Thrive Club* have actually built our own fallout shelters on our properties to keep our families safe because the government won't do that for us!"

A cheer of support filled the room.

"An atomic bomb attack from the Russians is imminent, and we must do our part to save the human race. The lecture today is entitled 'tips to survive the bomb' and I think you are going to enjoy our special guest. Please give a warm welcome to John Simmons from the California Civil Defense League."

There was enthusiastic applause as a man in his late fifties approached the podium. He had an obvious military bearing with short, cropped sandy-blond hair and a crisply ironed white short-sleeved shirt and black tie. On the chalkboard behind him someone, probably Mr. Simmons, had written *How To Survive An Atomic Attack*. Beside the heading there was a well-drawn caricature of Russian President Nikita Khrushchev standing with a pointer stick as if to display the different points that were obviously going to be written under the main heading.

"Hello, ladies and gentlemen," Mr. Simmons began, his voice gravelly and authoritative. He turned and gestured toward the drawing, "And hello, Mr. Khrushchev, glad you could attend." A hearty collective chuckle responded to the joke.

"I want to first address three common falsehoods about atomic bombs." Mr. Simmons paused, expertly catching the eyes of everyone in the room, his expression grave. He held Rosa's gaze a moment longer than any of the others, and Rosa suspected that she lacked a certain look possessed by other members of this club, namely her clothing. For this occasion she wore a white cotton dress with a strawberry pattern, a matching red pillbox hat and red patent leather shoes. Everyone else wore utilitarian fare, trousers and shirts with sneakers or boots. Two-inch pumps probably weren't of much use in the apocalypse. Rosa hadn't expected to be attending a Survive and Thrive meeting when she left the Forrester mansion.

With flourish, Mr. Simmons continued. "Number one, thanks to a weak government, we have no defense against atomic bombs. Number two, food hit by atomic rays is poisoned, which means those who are unprepared, if they don't die of radiation, will die of starvation. Number three, atomic rays kill everything they touch, so we must be ready to spend months—maybe years, in our bunkers. I hope you see how important a well-designed, well-equipped bunker is for survival. Now is not the time to skimp."

Rosa suspected that Mr. Simmons was the salesman and supplier for the equipment. Was he purposely benefiting from the fears he was personally instigating? Or did he honestly believe the hype and was sincere in his desire to help?

Glancing at her wristwatch, Rosa wondered how

long this lecture would go on for. She was glad that she had decided to leave Diego at the office, as sitting through a lecture would have been difficult with him no doubt squirming to escape her satchel the whole time.

After addressing these three main points, Mr. Simmons went on to discuss topics such as *six survival tricks* and *five keys to household safety*.

The lecture lasted about forty-five minutes and when it was over Mr. Simmons received a standing ovation. The host of the evening got up and after thanking the speaker, he gestured towards the snack table at the back and said, "Please help yourselves to our refreshments. Mr. Simmons is here to answer any questions you might have, and to take orders. Stick around and get to know your fellow survival enthusiasts."

Rosa made her way to the front to speak to John Raymond. He resembled a slim version of Santa Claus, except instead of wearing red he wore a blue cotton shirt with a bolero tie. If Santa Claus were from New Mexico, Rosa thought.

He turned to Rosa as she approached. "Well now, we don't get too many young ladies like yourself out to our meetings. Glad to see you." He extended his hand.

"Thank you." Rosa shook his hand. "I'm Miss Rosa

Reed, formerly of the London Metropolitan Police but I'm now… "

"London police!" Mr. Raymond took a step back. His mouth made an O shape as he raised his hands as if a gun were pointed at him, his bushy white eyebrows rising halfway up his forehead. "You finally found me, you blighters!" It was a very poor approximation of a British accent, and he knew it. His eyes twinkled with merriment.

Rosa couldn't help but chuckle. "Yes, very good. I will wait until later to put you in cuffs, though. We wouldn't want to start an international incident, would we?"

"Good idea." The man chuckled as he dropped his hands. "You'll have to excuse me. I spent some time in London during the last few months of the war. I got to know some 'Tommies' there and I appreciate the humor those boys all shared." He smiled again and then stroked his beard. "So, what brings a member of the London constabulary to our little meeting?"

"Actually, I'm living in Santa Bonita now. I work as a private detective. Do you have a moment we could talk?"

"Of course." The man's expression grew more serious. He gestured to a small round table, one of a dozen or so that had been placed in the room for people to sit and talk at while enjoying their refreshments.

"I'm wondering if you know someone named Dieter Braun," Rosa asked.

"Sure, I know Dieter! Everyone at our club does." He paused for a moment. "Why? Is he in some kind of trouble?"

"I am afraid there's been an incident out at his cabin on Lake Fairbanks."

"Oh?" Mr. Raymond's eyes expressed concern. "What kind of incident?"

"I'm afraid he's dead."

"How...what?"

"I'm sorry, but that's all I can tell you right now until the police have finished with the investigation. I have been hired by the Gainer family to look into the matter."

Mr. Raymond looked around the room as if searching for some kind of explanation. He seemed sincerely shaken by the news.

"I don't know what to say, Miss Reed. That's truly terrible news. Dieter Braun was one of us."

"Mr. Raymond, do you know if Dieter had any enemies? Anyone who might want to harm him?"

At the question, his eyes focused back on Rosa. "Harm him? Does that mean he was murdered?"

"As I said, it's an ongoing investigation."

The poor man reached for the nearest empty chair and lowered himself into it. After a moment he said,

"No, not at all. Dieter was very well liked here. He was a bit odd, yes, but some would say we are all a little odd in our club."

"How many members are in this club?"

"Usually twelve of us. Today is a bit different because we sponsored this lecture with Mr. Simmons."

"Was Mr. Braun usually at these meetings?"

"Usually, yes."

"And to your knowledge there is no one in the club who had anything against him?

"No, I don't think so."

"How about anybody who was especially close to him? Maybe a best friend within the group?"

"Not that I can think of. Dieter was gregarious enough, but I don't know if anyone really became close to him."

"When was the last time you saw him at a meeting?"

"Two weeks ago. He was supposed to be at our planning meeting on Tuesday night but didn't show."

"Do you know why?"

"Yeah, he called me early that afternoon. Apparently his Land Rover was acting up, and he needed to do some work on it. He was going to try and make it but if he didn't show up we were to go ahead without him."

"Was there anyone else missing from the meeting?"

"Nope. We were all there."

"What time did the meeting start?"

"We started at four. I supplied steaks and beer for everyone that night. When that happens, you can be sure no one shows up a minute late."

His eyes watered as he stared back at Rosa. "I was certain Dieter would make it for that, poor fella."

10

The next reasonable line of attack was to examine Dieter's Land Rover which was parked at the scene of the crime. Rosa was loathe to take her new Corvette on those gravel roads, so she borrowed a far more suitable jeep from the Forrester collection of vehicles. She rarely took advantage of Aunt Louisa's insistence that she borrow whatever vehicle she liked whenever she wanted, but today was an exception. Diego, her only companion, slept happily in her large satchel.

Stepping out of the vehicle, Rosa let Diego roam around under her watchful eye. After he'd spent enough time nosing around a grouping of wild ferns, Rosa scooped him back up into the satchel and walked past the cabin to the bunker. She was relieved to find the Land Rover unmoved. Rosa knew she had risked the wasting of several hours, driving all the way to the cabin just to find that the police had towed the vehicle off the property, but she couldn't very well have rung up Miguel and asked.

As it was, she could proceed with her investigation of the Land Rover as planned. No doubt Officer Richardson had taken photos, but it didn't appear as if anything had been altered or removed by the police.

Wearing gloves, Rosa opened the unlocked Land Rover and did a thorough search. An empty backpack and an unopened package of toilet paper sat in the back. On the floor, was another bit of tobacco, which she collected between her fingertips and sniffed.

Stashed under the seat was a toolbox. Rosa slid it out, opened it, and noted the contents. She then released the back hatch of the vehicle. It looked recently vacuumed, but she did find pine needles on the floor. She squinted at several small brown spots—blood? Rosa retrieved her camera and took pictures.

The keys hung in the ignition. Sliding into the driver's seat, Rosa started the engine. It caught right away but ran rather roughly. Rosa had to feed it more fuel to keep it idling constantly. Dieter hadn't been lying when he'd told Mr. Raymond his vehicle was running poorly. She guessed that one of the four cylinders was misfiring and the engine badly needed a tune-up. Like her mother, Rosa had a good working knowledge of mechanics. Engines were so delightfully logical. If there was a problem, one had to only go through the list of evidence, and eventually, the solution would be found. There were virtually no mysteries in mechanical work if one had the patience to track down each clue.

Rosa found the latch that opened the engine compartment and looked inside. She saw nothing out of the ordinary—the belts, the spark plug wires, and radiator hoses—but she did find a spark plug wrench wedged between the battery and the firewall. *Someone must have accidentally dropped it down there*?

Rosa collected her satchel, rousing Diego who gave her a narrow-eyed look of annoyance, and walked back to the jeep. The sun's rays glimmered over the lake's surface, and Rosa was delighted with the beauty of nature all around her. Birds, nesting in pine trees that were unbelievably tall, chirped happily while squirrels scampered up the trunks, releasing loose chips of bark that plummeted to the ground.

The red rowboat fastened to the dock caught Rosa's attention, and she instinctively headed down the wooden jetty instead.

"Shall we go for a spin, Diego?" Rosa untied the boat and carefully climbed in, putting the satchel on the wooden seat in front of her where she could keep an eye on Diego. However, the kitten seemed unwilling to venture out into the suddenly rocking outside world. His shining eyes peered out from the darkness of the bag.

"Good boy, Diego," Rosa murmured. "I can guess that a cat like you wouldn't exactly make a good pirate." She chuckled at the sight of his furry nose sticking out and sniffing the air. "A buccaneer worth his weight in gold has to battle things like raging seas and stormy gales, but even on these calm inland waters, it might be wise for the likes of you to stay below decks."

Rosa had a lot of experience with small craft, often rowing on the River Thames as a young girl with her father. The experience on this day was simply glorious. The sun was warm on her skin, the mountain air crisp and clean, and the small lake calm. The oars stirring the crystal-clear water and the call of a loon from across the lake were the only sounds.

"Wonderful."

Her repose came to a sudden halt when she spotted the forms of Miguel and Detective Sanchez walking slowly out onto the dock. They both stopped at the end and looked out at her. Detective Sanchez took off his hat and, after a moment, tentatively waved it at her while Miguel stood with his hands on his hips. She wasn't too surprised to see them. Though the body had been removed, there was still investigative work to be done here. She waved slowly, exactly the way she'd seen their new queen do, her hand slightly cupped and her palm barely pivoting on her wrist.

Miguel did not wave back.

Rosa sighed and kept rowing. Miguel was upset that she hadn't stopped by the precinct to share what she knew. Unfortunately, now that Rosa was working for Orville Gainer, and trying to protect Miguel's job, she couldn't do that. Not yet, at any rate.

Besides, Miguel would likely figure out the same things she had on his own.

Rosa navigated to the middle of the lake and scanned the shoreline. She could just make out a lone cabin and a small wooden dock on the east side of the lake. The cabin was barely visible from Dieter Braun's dock. She pointed the rowboat toward it. As she got closer, she saw a man on the edge of the dock in a chair, studying her with binoculars.

"Bingo," she said out loud.

Rosa rowed the boat nearer to the dock, stopping just short of the end, then called out, "Hello."

He was an elderly man with a grizzled face and a ring of gray hair peeking out from a straw hat. Rocking in a wooden chair with a tobacco-pipe holder and ashtray built into one of the arms, the man wore a white T-shirt, faded blue jeans, and sandals. A fishing rod and a tackle box lay on the dock, unopened.

"Beautiful day, isn't it?" she added.

"It sure is, young lady." The neighbor's voice was cheerful. "I'm guessing from the way you talk that you're not from around here." His leathered face was open and friendly with a large bushy mustache that all but covered his mouth.

"No, I'm originally from London, but I live in Santa Bonita now."

"Uh-huh." The man regarded her with a bit of puzzlement. "Are you a friend of that German fellow that lives there on the south end of the lake?"

"No, my name is Miss Rosa Reed. I'm a private detective."

"Name's John, John Givens. A lady gumshoe, huh? You don't see that much."

"I suppose not," Rosa said. "I am afraid there's been an incident involving Mr. Braun."

"Oh gosh, is he all right?"

"I am afraid not. The police are investigating his death right now."

"Sorry to hear it, Miss Reed." The man looked baffled as he took off his cap to scratch his head.

"Were you here when that earthquake hit last week?" Rosa asked.

"Yes, ma'am. I've been out here for a month, but I got to tell you, I never felt a thing. I heard about it on the news, though. I get good radio reception out here most days."

"How many other cabins are there on the lake?" Rosa asked.

"Just the Braun fellow's place and mine. There are a few private properties, but no one has built anything, though I am sure that will come soon enough. I built this cabin here just after my wife died twelve years ago. I was the only one until Braun built his.

"I only spoke to him a couple times when he was building it. Our types tend to keep to ourselves. But I saw him a few times out there on the lake with that boat you've commandeered." He gestured towards the rowboat and smiled to let her know he was teasing her the way cheery old men often do. "He always gave me a wave because he knew I was watching him through my binoculars."

"When was the last time you saw him?"

Mr. Givens took off his hat and scratched his head. "Just last week. Maybe five days ago. In the evening, as I recall. I only noticed because he had a flashlight, and the beam flashed about as he paced his dock."

"Why do you think he would walk out on the dock after dark?" Rosa asked.

"I confess to looking through my binoculars–it's the only entertainment I have out here–and I could swear he threw something into the lake."

"Any ideas?"

He shrugged a bony shoulder. "Well, it looked like some kind of tool, 'bout a foot and a half long."

"Could it have been a hammer?"

"Well, that's kind of what I thought at the time. But why would Mr. Braun walk his dock in the dead of night and toss a hammer into the water? Even with a flashlight, a fellow could misstep and fall in."

"Are you sure it was Mr. Braun?"

More head scratching. "To be honest, I couldn't see his face. But who else would it be?"

Rosa was thinking the same.

"Whatever it was," the neighbor said, "he must've known he could retrieve it later, most likely. It's only about five feet deep that distance from shore."

Rosa thanked the man for his time, then rowed back to Dieter Braun's dock. Her stomach clenched at the sight of Miguel—if he'd left at any point, he had returned and stood waiting for her.

"Have a nice voyage?" His voice sounded gruff. He grabbed the rope she tossed him, tied it to the dock post, and helped her step out. A shiver rolled through Rosa at his touch. She didn't like being that close to him. Mostly because she *loved* being near him. She could smell his aftershave, which made her pulse quicken. Holding her breath, she stepped away.

"Aha... Deputy Diego is also on the scene," Miguel said with a note of mirth.

"You might want to get a diver out here," Rosa said, taking another step back.

Miguel frowned at the growing distance but didn't try to close the gap. "Why do you say that?"

"I don't know how far you are in your investigation yet, but—"

"I am treating it as a homicide."

Rosa lifted her chin. "The head wound?"

"Yes, and a few other things I am not at liberty to ..."

Rosa interrupted. "The effects of that earthquake last week were not felt here at all."

"Yes, I know, we checked it out already. How...?"

"You'll find the murder weapon, a framing hammer probably with the initials DB scratched into it, just off the end of the dock. Snorkeling equipment will suffice since the water is only five feet deep there."

"What? Wait."

"A nice old man is living in a cabin on the east side of the lake. You might want to interview him, but I doubt he would be a suspect." Rosa walked away.

Miguel lengthened his gait and fell in beside her. "C'mon Rosa, what's up?"

Rosa felt torn. She already felt like she'd given him too much. She couldn't risk him solving the murder before she could, and he already had the advantage of Detective Sanchez and the coroner's office helping him, while she was on her own. She didn't care who solved the case, but despite the Gainer family stonewalling him, if Miguel got too close too fast, or asked too many questions, it could mean his job. Rosa turned to say something but then decided to keep walking.

"Rosa!" Miguel shouted after her. "Are you still investigating for the Gainers?"

Drat! Miguel's nose for the truth is in tip-top shape.

"I'm sorry, Miguel. I'm in a terrible hurry. We can catch up another time."

Rosa hopped into the jeep, started the engine, and cautiously drove away. Diego hopped out of the satchel, leaped onto the warm dashboard, and sprawled out languidly as if he hadn't a care in the world.

11

Alice Monahan had agreed to meet Rosa at the Chug Away Diner, a converted railcar establishment, set inland amongst the sage and awkward-looking Joshua trees. The diner, long and narrow, had an abundance of chrome, black-and-white checkered flooring, and smelled of fried food and strong coffee. A row of barstools lined a long counter along one side. Rosa spotted Alice in one of the red vinyl booths that lined the other, looking nervous and holding a half-empty mug. Rosa slid into the seat across from her. The diner was not the type of place Rosa pictured Mrs. Monahan frequenting and could only assume the place had been chosen so none of her circle would chance seeing them together.

"Thanks for agreeing to meet," Rosa said. It was the first time they had really spoken together personally other than a brief conversation at the first Gainer gathering. Though Mrs. Monahan hadn't been married to Dieter Braun, she was the sister of the woman who had been. Perhaps Lillian Braun had confided in her sister about her marriage before she passed away. It was a long shot, but Rosa didn't like to leave any stone unturned.

A waitress dressed in a red-and-white uniform arrived with a pot of coffee, and Rosa positioned the clean mug on a paper placemat, upright.

"Thank you," she said, accepting the offer of cream and sugar.

"Menus?" the waitress asked.

Mrs. Monahan answered. "That won't be necessary. We're not staying long."

The waitress shrugged. "Suit yourself."

In her mid-fifties, Mrs. Monahan was reasonably slim and attractive. Her blue eyes, though saddened by grief, were still bright and lively. Her hair, which she wore in a tidy bouffant, showed signs of gray at her temples.

"I confess, I can't understand why you wanted to speak to me," Mrs. Monahan said. "I only agreed to meet with you because I'm terribly curious by nature. That, and the fact that Orville insisted we all talk to you if asked."

Rosa found the flippant use of her father's given name a matter to note.

"I do appreciate you taking the time," Rosa said. "How well did you know your brother-in-law?"

Alice Monahan's gaze widened with a glint of suspicion. "What do you mean?"

Rosa had expected a general response; now, she wondered if there was a reason the lady was inexplicably defensive.

"I only mean, did your sister ever confide in you about her relationship with her husband."

Mrs. Monahan pursed her lips. "In our family, it's almost impossible to keep a secret."

"So then, you must know something about their marriage," Rosa stated.

"I don't see how this line of questioning is relevant. Honestly, I find it disrespectful."

"I mean no disrespect," Rosa said, "I assure you. I'm only trying to learn more about Mr. Braun and those who were close to him."

"So you can accuse one of us of murder?"

"I'm simply doing what Orville Gainer hired me to do."

Evoking her father's name seemed to take some of the wind out of the lady's sails.

"I can tell you what everyone will tell you. Dieter

didn't fit well into our family. Over time, it caused a rift to form between Lillian and Dieter."

"Can you explain why he didn't fit? What did that look like?"

"Dieter was a square peg trying to fit in a round hole. My brother Walter didn't trust him for reasons I am not sure of and my sister Valerie just thought he was crazy. My father detested him. He doesn't trust foreigners, especially Germans. With Dieter's accent, his mannerisms, and his conspiracy theories, well, he was barely tolerated."

Alice Monahan let out a mournful sigh. "I didn't blame him for wanting to hide out at his cabin. If I could escape this family as easily, I would. After Lillian died, Dieter practically lived at the lake full time. He conducted his insurance business by telephone.

"What kind of insurance did he sell, exactly?" Rosa asked.

Alice Monahan lifted a slender shoulder. "I wouldn't know. All kinds, I think."

Rosa sipped on her coffee. "What about you? How did you feel about Dieter Braun?"

Mrs. Monahan's eyes softened. "Honestly? I liked him. I admired his spunk and the way he stood up to my father without saying a word. He *was* a bit strange, though, always talking about aliens, Soviet invasions, and the like. But he also was a hard worker and a very shrewd businessman. Anyway, Lillian told me about his bomb shelter, but I've never seen it."

"Do you know if anyone else from the family has ever been out there?"

"Anyone could've driven to the cabin. I have no way of knowing that." She turned to look directly at Rosa. "But I know you want to ask me who I thought would ever want to murder Dieter."

Rosa *did* want to ask that. "Who *do* you think killed Mr. Braun?"

Mrs. Monahan gazed out of the diner window at the desert landscape, as if lost in thought. After a moment, she looked at Rosa. "Leo Romano. No one hated him more than Leo. I hate to rat out my sister's husband, but he seemed to blame Dieter for the First World War personally. Leo fought in the battle of Belleau Wood against the Germans, as did his older brother Gino. Unfortunately, Gino was killed by a German soldier in hand-to-hand combat. According to army records, both soldiers had run out of bullets. Gino was killed by several blows to the head with the stock of the German's gun."

Rosa fought to hold her expression at the grim description.

"Dieter didn't even know Leo had a brother," Mrs. Monahan continued. "Then, one night at a family party, Dieter had too much to drink. He usually abstained and for good reason, but on that night, he got carried away."

Her gaze latched on to Rosa's, and she sighed again. "I'm only telling you this because you're bound to hear about it anyway. That night, Dieter started talking about World War One. What a foolish, *foolish* thing to do! Turns out, he was in Belleau Wood on that exact day. And even though the German offenses were thwarted in that battle, he bragged about killing an American soldier in close hand-to-hand combat. Well, of course, Leo was incensed! He was convinced that Dieter had killed Gino, though there's no way to know it for sure."

Mrs. Monahan sipped her coffee, most probably cold by now, and grimaced. She pushed the mug to the side. "Leo threw a punch at Dieter. Frank and Colin had to hold him back. We tried to tell him that both wars were long over and that there was a slim chance it was his brother anyways, but Leo wouldn't listen. Vowing he would pay Dieter back someday, he stormed out of the party."

"When did this happen exactly?"

"About a month ago."

Alice Monahan paid for their coffees and then made a hasty departure. As the diner was on the same side of town as Leo Romano's latest construction venture, Rosa decided that now might be a good time to head over.

Surrounded by scaffolding and heavy equipment, at least two dozen workers buzzed around a four-story-high cement structure wearing yellow safety hats and work boots. A crane lifted lumber to a waiting crew on the top level. An artist's rendering of an apartment complex posted on the wire fence had a logo with the words: *Romano Construction—Santa Bonita's Partner for the Future.* The construction site radiated frenetic energy.

Leo Romano was at his desk in his makeshift office trailer. A stack of blueprints and the largest coffee thermos Rosa had ever seen were surrounded by a mess of papers. He stared at Rosa with a look of dismay, then exhaled in defeat, as if he knew it would be less trouble to talk to her than to try to send her away without giving her what she had come for.

"Please have a seat." He gestured to a rough wooden chair sitting opposite the desk, pushed up from his chair, and shut the door. The noise coming from a jackhammer operating somewhere at the far end of the construction site became muffled. One entire wall of the trailer was covered in blueprints and technical drawings. Another had a large window with a good view of the building site.

Leo Romano leaned back in his leather office chair

and weaved his fingers together over a rounded belly. "Well, I suppose you wouldn't be worth your salt as an investigator if the trail didn't come to me at the outset."

"Half the Gainer clan heard you utter threats toward Dieter Braun," Rosa said.

"Yes. I suppose the family members are all looking at me with suspicion and animosity right now." With a chuckle, he added, "But that hasn't changed from day one."

Rosa took out her notepad, "What do you mean?"

"I married into a family of snakes, and now our daughter is engaged to one of them. Inbreeding! But those Gainers like to keep things in-house. A den of secrets, I tell you. Most of which I don't even know, so you're not likely going to learn much from me."

He pointed at her notepad. "I'd appreciate it if you didn't quote me on that."

"These are for my personal use," Rosa said. "I understand you had a brother who died in the First World War?"

Mr. Romano's brow formed deep crevices. "I'm sure I'm not alone in that regard."

"Is it true that you blamed Dieter Braun for your brother's death?"

A twitch of the lips. "That, my dear girl, was a moment of whiskey-infused passion. What are the odds that the German who killed my brother would immigrate to California and marry my wife's sister?"

"Rather low, I suspect," Rosa admitted. "However, if one believed it to be true, it could drive one to take matters into one's own hands."

Mr. Romano pressed his hands onto his desk and leaned in. "Might I give you a piece of advice, Miss Reed?"

"If you must." Rosa doubted she could stop him if she tried.

"Here in California, we don't have a queen. If you plan to stick around, you will do well to try to sound like one of us."

Rosa ground her teeth then repeated her statement. "If *you* believed it to be your brother, it might drive you to take matters into your own hands."

Chuckling, Mr. Romano said, "As much as I despised Braun, I didn't kill him." He removed a package of cigarettes from his shirt pocket, flamed the tip of one, and deeply inhaled. With a fast exhale, he released a plume of smoke into the small area. "Forgive me for being blunt, Miss Reed, but I'm glad he's dead and gone. Now that Lillian has passed away, there's no one left to mourn him."

"Janet Gainer seemed rather fond of him."

"*Rather*," Mr. Romano repeated with a note of mockery. "She's got a soft heart. The kind that likes to feed stray dogs and cats." After a pause, he added, "And a stray German."

Rosa pressed on. "Have you ever been out to Mr. Braun's cabin?"

"No, and by the way, my wife and I have an alibi. We were on vacation for two weeks in Florida at the time that earthquake hit last week." He took another puff of his cigarette. "We only got back the morning of that gathering where you masqueraded as a niece of Janet's friend. I can provide plane ticket stubs, hotel, rental car receipts, and the phone number of my sister. We were with them the entire time."

Rosa made a note to check with Janet about the Romanos' travel itinerary.

"Now, if I were you," Leo Romano, docked his cigarette on an ashtray, leaned back in his chair, and clasped his hands behind his head. "I would be looking at Frank Monahan."

"Why is that?"

"Very recently, Frank found out that his wife, Alice, was having an affair with good old Dieter. Apparently, Dieter was doing more than fishing and building a bomb shelter at that cabin."

Rosa blinked. Alice Monahan was the only Gainer family member who hadn't spoken disparagingly about Mr. Braun, but that didn't mean they'd been having an affair.

"How do you know this is true?" Rosa asked.

"Frank and I aren't pals, but on occasion, we go for a beer to commiserate over our shared misfortune of being connected to the Gainer clan. His marriage to Alice was never a good one. After a few, he got it off his chest. He'd been suspicious about his wife's behavior for a while and followed her one day while she thought he was at work. Imagine his surprise when she took that long drive to Lake Fairbanks!

"When he confronted Alice later that day, she admitted it, saying she was in love with Dieter and wanted a divorce."

Leo Romano crookedly grinned as he readied to lower the final blow. "Frank's a proud man. There was no way he was going to let that happen."

12

After leaving the construction site, Rosa headed down the Pacific Coast Highway. The sunlight sparkling in the ocean, the wind blowing in her face, and the thrumming of the Corvette's engine vibrating through her bones, Rosa found the open road a soothing distraction from this puzzling case.

As she drove north, the highway split into four lanes. At the last traffic light, while waiting for the light to turn green, the roar of an engine accentuated with the bass line of a song playing loudly on a car's radio, approached from behind. A shiny, deep-blue, older-model Roadster rolled up beside her. Rosa guessed the vehicle was a 1930's Ford, but it had been meticulously restored and modified. Clarence had called a similar car a *hot rod*.

The powerful, rumbling engine was completely exposed to reveal a chrome air filter and valve covers. The driver pumped the engine twice, and when Rosa glanced over, she was stunned to see Colin Monahan waving casually. A mischievous grin formed on his face, and his eyes had a wild look as he peered at her over the top of his dark sunglasses. Hatless, a good amount of hair oil kept all but his duckbill from blowing out of place.

The music of Carl Perkins, singing about blue suede shoes, blared through the radio. Colin Monahan revved his engine again, and the whole car rocked. His intent was clear.

Rosa felt adrenaline flood her system. A smile tugged at her mouth as she looked straight ahead, pumped her accelerator, and answered the Roadster with the Corvette's thunderous growl. They were like two mythical beasts eager to be unleashed from their cages and to wreak havoc upon the town of Santa Bonita.

The light turned green, and both vehicles sprang ahead from the intersection amidst the deafening roar of unshackled horsepower and the squeal of burning tire rubber. The Roadster fishtailed ahead while Rosa gently took the pressure off the accelerator and allowed the car to peak at the posted speed limit, a demure forty miles per hour.

Rosa chuckled. No one was going to dictate to the daughter of Ginger Gold when it was time to let the horses out of the gate.

Besides, it was almost time for tea.

As the Roadster disappeared recklessly around a bend, Rosa thought of the nice café she had seen on her last drive this way called the *Red House Coffee and Brewing Company*. A sign along the highway boasted that the establishment carried its own brand of coffee *and* beer plus various pastries and burgers. A few minutes later, the café came into view, and Rosa was surprised to see Colin Monahan there, stepping toward the front entrance. He stopped when he saw her drive in, then leaned against his car with his arms crossed. Rosa pulled the Corvette to a stop in the parking lot next to him.

"You seemed to be in a frightful hurry to get here," Rosa said in mock seriousness as she stepped out of her car. "Is there a special on croissants or something?"

"Ha. You're funny." One corner of Colin Monahan's mouth pulled upward into a half-smile. "What's the matter?" He spread his hands in front of himself, gesturing to the Corvette. "Are you afraid your baby ain't got what it takes to burn some good rubber?"

"Well, if you must know," Rosa began, "I was being kind. Your funny little car is cute, but...well, let's just say it lacks the dominant pedigree that my motorcar has."

"Ho, ho!" Colin Monahan laughed. "*Dominant pedigree*? You're a piece of work!" He gestured toward the café. "I think you should join me. They serve great craft beer here."

"Do they serve tea?"

He laughed. "Tea? Ha, that's a good one!"

Rosa's expression was without humor as she lowered her sunglasses to look at him.

"Oh, you're serious…um…" Colin Monahan cleared his throat, "Sure, they must have tea. *Maybe* even English muffins and crumpets." His chuckle caught in his throat.

Rosa was happy to accept. She'd been wondering how she would wrangle an interview with Orville Gainer's two grandsons and was thrilled with this serendipitous turn of events.

Colin claimed the booth next to the window, "Gotta keep an eye on my *chariot*."

Rosa noted a marked difference from the Colin Monahan she had met at the Gainer party the first time she was there, and the brash man sitting before her now. A leather jacket and blue jeans rolled to the ankles replaced the pressed suit and tie. At the party, he had been pensive and moody, almost reluctant to talk. Now he gave off a certain bravado and swagger and was rather flirtatious.

Shortly after they'd taken a seat, a cheerful waitress in a bright yellow uniform came to take their order.

"I would like a cup of Earl Grey tea," Rosa said.

The waitress pulled a pencil that was tucked behind her ear and grinned. "It's just plain black tea, sugar."

"I'll take black tea with milk."

Colin Monahan ordered a dark beer and French fries.

"So, tell me," Colin Monahan started. He folded his hands on the table and leaned forward. "How does a proper lady like yourself get involved in something like private investigative work?"

Again, that sly smile, Rosa thought. He wasn't truly interested in her background; he was making a pass at her. A rich young bachelor like Mr. Monahan was probably used to obtaining any hapless girl he chose to toy with. Rosa was not so easily impressed, but she could play the game when it suited her purpose.

She allowed a flirtatious smile. "I'll tell you that story if you tell me yours first."

Colin Monahan cocked his head sideways and hesitated. "Well, I guess that's your job, isn't it? You were probably planning to question me sometime soon anyway, I figure. I just saved you a phone call, didn't I?"

Rosa was saved from answering when the waitress arrived with their orders.

Colin Monahan smirked. "And you get your cup of tea and cookie too!"

Rosa raised an eyebrow then blew on her tea.

"Ha! Okay, fire away, Sherlock. What do you want to know?"

"Where were you last Tuesday night, the night Dieter Braun was murdered?"

"Right to the point, huh?" After wolfing down several fries and following that with a long swig of beer, he answered. "Well, if you have to know, I was up on Caesar's Point with a girl."

"Caesar's Point?"

"It's a lookout spot south of town off the main highway. A lot of young people go up there to, ah, well it's kind of a make out spot. Backseat bingo if you get my drift."

Rosa had seen and heard a lot of vulgar things in her line of work and was unruffled by her companion's brashness.

She challenged him. "You're a little old for that, aren't you?"

"I wasn't aware of an age limit. Making out under the stars overlooking the ocean never gets dull."

"Were you in your, er, Roadster?" Rosa nodded toward the blue hot rod sitting in the parking lot.

"Nah, not enough privacy. Jenny has a nice Oldsmobile."

Rosa took out her notebook. "Jenny…"

"Ah, ya, I don't remember her last name, sorry."

Rosa stared back.

"*Whaaat?* I met her at a bar in Schofield earlier that night. She's a nice girl. Nice figure too."

"What's her phone number?" Rosa lifted her pen to write.

Colin just shrugged his shoulders. Rosa sighed.

"Either it's me or the police who will be talking to her."

"I think she said she was here visiting friends. She's from out of town." He squinted as if remembering a long-forgotten detail.

"What friends?"

"I think she knows the bartender where we met. I don't know his name, offhand."

"Which bar?" Rosa was getting impatient.

"Yeah, which one was it now? Oh ya, *The Tanker*."

"What time were you there at the bar?"

"I think around eight, stayed until around ten, and then Jenny and I left."

"Did you speak to anyone besides Jenny?"

Colin sipped his beer, then said, "Nah."

"Was your Roadster parked in the parking lot?" Rosa tilted her head and stared with an expression she imagined was worn by frustrated teachers across the nation. "In other words, can anyone other than Jenny with no last name and no phone number or known address vouch for you?"

Colin sniggered. "I see what you're getting at. But, no, I parked down the road in front of Ralph's supermarket. There is a lot of lighting in that huge lot. Less chance of someone scratching the paint."

"Was there anyone else at Caesar's Point?"

"I don't know." Colin grinned. "The windows were kind of steamy."

"If I were you," Rosa said, "I would think hard if you saw anyone or if anyone saw you. Right now, you have a very weak alibi."

With the money at Colin's disposal, Rosa knew Colin could buy off a bartender to say he was at the bar. Besides that, it would be a job trying to find witnesses that might have seen his hot rod parked at the supermarket after opening hours.

"Why, Miss Reed," Colin said, his crooked smile returning, "I think that you believe I make a good suspect."

Rosa watched him intently. There was a flash of something that showed in his eyes. She wasn't sure if it was anger or fear.

Undaunted, she said, "Tell me about your relationship with the rest of the Gainers."

Colin rolled his eyes. "That was the first question the police asked me this morning too. You detective types need to update your playbook."

Rosa took a sip of tea and grimaced. She'd been so busy questioning Colin Monahan that her drink had cooled.

Colin took her silence as mute disapproval. "Okay, okay. I have been *instructed* to cooperate with you," he said with some sarcasm. "I wouldn't want word getting back to the old man that I didn't answer *all* of your questions. I get along fine enough with just about everybody. I mean, my dad's Irish as you know, and though Grandpa would've preferred a British bloodline, it's as near as acceptable as you can get in this clan. More palatable than say, Romano. Or even worse, Braun."

"Have you worked with any of the Gainers in your business?" Rosa asked. "Import and export, perhaps?"

"Sidney and I did some work together. I thought maybe that would work out well."

"It didn't?"

Colin finished the last of his fries then wiped his mouth with a napkin. "It's funny, you know, when we were kids, we were close. He was almost like an older brother. We both learned to sail on my grandpa's yacht.

We would go out on excursions together as teenagers." He grinned in that infuriating way. "We were popular with the girls."

He paused as he reflected then said, "When Sidney hit his adult years, he turned into such a drag."

"It didn't work out in business, then?" Rosa asked.

Colin stared into his beer glass.

Rosa pressed. "Your grandfather promised me that I would have access to all the financial records of the various businesses too."

That seemed to catch Colin by surprise. He looked up at her and quickly drank down the remainder of his beer. "Oh, really?" He tapped his fingers on the side of his beer glass. "Well then, I suppose you would find out that my import and export business hasn't done so well. It was a good idea, but there were some, uh, unfortunate events that caused big setbacks. Sidney enlisted partners that didn't deliver on their promises." He snorted. "Sidney puts on a good show. He's all cool and suave while I am always the guy who gets into trouble. I'm always screwing up, it seems."

He sighed, showing a rare sign of vulnerability. "My dad is proud of me when I defend myself and get into a fistfight, but the old man at the top...well, he is downright disgusted, and he lets me know it. Says next time he'll let the police arrest me."

Rosa noted how Colin believed his grandfather had

a powerful sway with the police. She thought sourly that perhaps he did.

"Sidney's his blue-eyed boy," Colin continued. "Always gives the impression that he's got the world by the tail." He let out a scornful chuckle. "That's a big front."

"Oh?" Rosa said. "How so?"

"Whereas I have already proven that no matter what *I* do, I can't please the old man, Sidney can do no wrong." He looked away as he shook his head, his mouth turned down in a scornful scowl. "It's why I've stopped trying. If he thinks I'm a bad boy, then I'll be the bad boy."

Then he looked Rosa straight in the eye. "But Sidney's the good grandson, and he'd do anything to get and keep Grandpa's approval. *Anything*."

"What do you mean by that?"

Colin looked away again. "Nothing. Forget it." He pushed himself out of the booth. "It's been nice chattin' with you, Miss Reed." He smiled, but it was a sarcastic expression. "I suddenly realized that I have more important things to do today than sit and talk about the Gainer clan. No offense. You can report to old man Gainer that I was the perfect interviewee. Or not, I don't care."

Colin Monahan slipped on his sunglasses and with an air of defeat, took his leave.

13

Rosa's next stop was the Santa Bonita Hospital—more precisely the morgue. Stepping into the sterile-looking environment, she waved through the glass office window to Chief Medical Examiner Dr. Philpott. She couldn't stop her eyes from furtively searching for Larry.

"Hello, Miss Reed," Dr. Philpott said. The pathologist had a happy, Father Christmas type of appearance and demeanor that Rosa felt quite incongruous with his workplace and vocation.

"Hello, Dr. Philpott." As a private investigator, Rosa didn't have the authority to request information from either pathologist but hoped that she'd have some sway with Larry. Before, she'd only ever showed up with the support of Miguel and his badge.

"What can I do for you today?" Dr. Philpott said

with a twinkle in his eye. "No, let me guess, I'm not the pathologist you're looking for."

Word of Rosa and Larry going out on a few dates had clearly reached the man. His statement was true, if not for the reasons he suspected. She smiled.

"Is Dr. Rayburn in?"

"He's in his office. I'm sure you know the way."

Dr. Philpott chuckled at his joke as the offices of the two pathologists were side by side, then disappeared into his own.

Rosa knocked on Larry's office door.

"Com' on in, Rosa," he said.

Rosa opened the door and stepped inside. She smiled at Larry, who was seated at his desk, a pen in hand, and a stack of papers clearly in need of signing.

"I suppose you could hear all of that?" she said.

Larry waved to the walls. "Paper thin." Then louder, "Aren't they, Mel?"

Rosa couldn't help but chuckle. She took the chair facing Larry.

"I'm sorry to interrupt," Rosa said. "I'll only take a minute of your time."

Larry dropped his pen and locked her gaze. "For you, Miss Reed, I have all the time in the world."

Rosa felt herself blush. Larry Rayburn wasn't one to keep his feelings to himself, a trait rarely found among the British, especially the gentlemen folk. Rosa had a hard time adjusting to his transparency.

"I'm sorry," he said. "I've embarrassed you."

"Oh no," Rosa said, feeling newly embarrassed at the notion that Larry could read her discomfort on her face. "I'm just not used to blatant admiration." *At least not from anyone other than Miguel, once upon a time, a long time ago.*

Larry laughed. "I'll try to ease up then, but ya don't make it easy, ma'am."

Rosa laughed in return. "I'm here because I've been hired by Orville Gainer to look into the death of Dieter Braun."

The amusement in Larry's eyes faded. "I thought you were hired by Mrs. Janet Gainer to find Mr. Braun."

"Yes, but then, once I located his body, Mr. Orville Gainer engaged me."

"I see." Larry frowned. "Well, I'm fairly new to Santa Bonita, not even five years, but I've heard of the Gainer clan. You best be careful, Rosa."

"I intend to. At the moment, there's no reason for alarm. I'm simply fact-finding."

"And you want to know about certain facts that I have?"

"That's right."

"I can give what is considered general knowledge

in the hospital," Larry said. Rosa wondered if Miguel had beaten her to the punch and had cautioned Larry against giving her certain information.

Larry went on. "First of all, my estimation of the time of death is roughly between six p.m. and midnight Tuesday. That time frame is based on the usual factors: the degree of rigor mortis, the vitreous potassium level, lividity, stomach contents, etcetera."

Rosa was familiar with the forensic elements.

"As for the cause of death, well, I could tell straight off when I saw the body that it wasn't that fallin' shelf that killed him, though it caused a fracture of the hip and a rib."

"Hammer blow to the head?" Rosa ventured.

"A hammer is a very probable weapon. The injury to the skull is consistent with the claw end of a hammer. From the angle of the blow, I would say the killer is between five foot eight and five foot eleven in height if the blow was administered while both killer and victim were standing."

"That makes perfect sense."

"You know what else would make sense?"

Rosa lifted her chin, eager to hear anything that might help her move this case along. "What's that?"

Larry grinned. "You goin' out for dinner with me tonight."

That would be twice in three days. Rosa liked

Larry, but she'd just gotten out of a marital engagement and wasn't ready to jump into anything serious quite yet.

"I'm afraid my evening is already booked," she said lightly. "Can I take a rain check?"

The disappointment that flashed behind Larry's blue eyes was fleeting. He quickly recovered.

"Well, I'll have to check my calendar, Miss Reed." He made a show of looking at the calendar propped on his desk. "Ah, yes, anytime beyond tonight will work."

THE NEXT MORNING, after a wonderful breakfast of *huevos rancheros*, a Mexican-style omelet prepared by the ever-cheerful Señora Gomez, Rosa collected Diego in her satchel and headed for Santa Bonita pier. Sidney Gainer, under the arrangement Rosa had with Orville Gainer, had agreed to an interview before he left for San Diego on his yacht.

It was another lovely morning, and although it was only nine o'clock by the time Rosa arrived at the main boating dock, the sun was already warm. The luxury yacht was painted white with beautiful mahogany-brown trim and was equipped with a wonderful back deck for lounging. On the side of the boat, its name, *Conqueror,* was painted in black.

As Sidney Gainer helped Rosa step onboard,

Diego poked his head out of the satchel. "You brought a cat onto a boat?"

"Is that a bad idea?" Rosa asked. It hadn't occurred to her it might be. He had done fine on the rowboat on Lake Fairbanks. She'd left her cat to fend for himself most of the previous day and didn't want to do it two days in a row. "I mean, do you mind?"

"No, I don't mind at all, it's just that I don't have a life preserver that small." Sidney chuckled smoothly, and Rosa could see how his charm could work in his favor.

Rosa placed the satchel on the enclosed deck, and a few moments later, Diego gingerly stepped out. After sniffing around for a few seconds, he went directly to a spot where the sun was shining onto the wood floor and lay down.

Rosa smiled at her pet. "He'll be asleep in a moment. Nice boat, by the way."

"It's a fifty-three mahogany hull," Sidney Gainer proudly said as they sat down on the leather-padded bench seats on the rear deck. "Sleeps eight. I bought this particular model because I like the *flybridge* feature on it." Sidney pointed to the canvas-covered station where the navigation and steering equipment was located. "On a nice day like today, I can take off the canvas and open the front window to let the wind in while I am driving. I like the feeling of being high up off the waves. If I leave soon, I'll be in San Diego by nightfall. I don't know if Grandpa told you, but I'm a seafaring man. You'll never find me on an airplane."

"I flew here from London, via New York," Rosa said. "It was a rather pleasant experience, like dining in a fine restaurant thousands of feet in the air. I got here all in one day!"

"If I can't get somewhere by boat or by train, I don't go. This baby has twin 440 gas-powered inboard engines. Plenty of zip." He pointed to the floor. "The decks are teakwood!"

"How far *can* you go on a vessel like this?" Rosa asked.

"I suppose you could go anywhere. I have a place in Baja, Mexico, that I like to visit, and from there I could go down to South America if I wanted. A person could sail around the world if he carried enough fuel on board to get him across the big seas. Maybe I'll do that someday. Out of all the Gainers, I suppose I am the only one with a *truly* adventurous spirit. Always looking over the horizon, always searching for kingdoms to conquer. That's why the boat is named *Conqueror*."

Sidney looked out at the horizon as if hearing the call of untamed lands in the distance that were waiting to welcome him as a victorious king.

Rosa had to avoid laughing at such ostentatiousness. This man was in love with himself, which reminded her of Debbie Romano.

"What does your future wife think about such adventures?"

Sidney Gainer shrugged. "We haven't talked about it. If she doesn't want to join me, she doesn't have to."

"Forgive me for saying so, but you don't sound like a man in love."

Sidney scoffed. "This is a marriage of convenience. Why do you think I'm getting married to my cousin?"

"I wouldn't know. It's why I'm asking."

Sidney was an attractive man in his early-thirties, and Rosa was certain there would be a lineup of ladies ready to sign on to the luxurious life that would belong to Mrs. Sidney Gainer.

Unless, of course, Mr. Sidney Gainer wasn't interested in women?

Not Rosa's business.

Sidney crossed his legs and removed his sunglasses. Staring at Rosa, he said, "You didn't come here to talk about boats nor my engagement. And yes, I know Grandpa said we are to cooperate, so ask away."

"A boat like this must cost a lot of money," Rosa said. "What type of business are you engaged in?"

"Well, you're direct, aren't you?"

"I get the feeling you are in a hurry to be off, so I thought I should get to the heart of the matter."

"I'm a real estate speculator, like my grandfather, I or I should say we—Grandpa is not quite retired—have projects here in the USA and Asia."

"What about your cousin Colin?" Rosa purposefully left the question open-ended.

"Colin's a hothead. Always getting into trouble, always trying to prove himself in one way or another. And when it comes to business, he just doesn't have the mind for it. Takes after Uncle Frank in that respect. Against my better judgment, I tried to help him with his import company, but he just simply doesn't have the patience or the people skills."

"I saw his hot rod," Rosa said. "Where does he get the money for an expensive vehicle if he's not in the real estate game like you and some of the others?"

"His mother, my Aunt Alice, feels sorry for him. He's also got a trust fund. All the grandkids do."

"What was your relationship like with Dieter Braun?"

"You mean, did I kill Uncle Dieter?"

"Okay, if you like. What were you doing last Tuesday evening?"

"I was at Grandpa's place. Debbie was with me, as well. We were watching television together as we often do on Tuesday nights."

Rosa sighed. That alibi would take some work to unravel if it was false.

"What did you watch?"

"A couple of shows, but the main event is always *Name That Tune.* A gal won forty clams for "Goodnight Irene". Anyways, I went to bed around ten. So, to answer your question, my relationship with Uncle Dieter was strained like it was with him and almost the whole family. He was an odd duck and never did fit in with the clan."

Rose pursed her lips in thought. Did any member of this family actually feel like they fitted in?

14

Frank and Alice Monahan lived in an upper-middle-class neighborhood in the north end. The street was the perfect picture of the typical *American dream* as Rosa had heard someone call it. The sun hung low on the horizon, and as she turned the Corvette onto the boulevard, she saw several children playing hopscotch on the smoothly paved road. Two men mowed their lawns, and another man played catch with a little boy in his front yard. As she drove by, the man took off his cap with one hand and pointed at the passing Corvette with the other. She heard him call to the boy, "See that, Thomas? That's my next car."

Diego poked his head out of the satchel. He was used to riding in the car with the top down now, and instead of burrowing deep inside the tapestry bag, he would stick his entire head out and sniff the air as they breezed along the road, that was if he hadn't struck his sunbathing pose on the dashboard. His young kitten awkwardness was fading, and he was growing quickly. With his new agility, he was even bolder at the Forrester mansion. Rosa brought him with her as often as she could to keep the peace with her Aunt Louisa, who had a rather tense relationship with Diego ever since he had damaged a panel of unique drapery, coughed up a hairball on an expensive rug, and scratched the teak trim of the sofa.

As a result, Rosa thought Diego needed some instruction, and after reading in a magazine about such a thing as cat training, she'd asked Gloria to search for a cat training school. *Deputy Diego,* as Miguel called him, was very smart for a cat, and usually well mannered, but it was as if he sensed Aunt Louisa's animosity and was determined to exploit it. The affair would be quite funny if Aunt Louisa weren't so testy. The whole house suffered when she got into one of her moods. Perhaps a professional could help Deputy Diego.

Rosa spied the house number on a row of impressive-looking homes, each with the address colorfully painted on a Spanish tile beside the front door. She pushed Diego back deeper into her satchel, wrapped the strap over her shoulder, and walked up the paved walkway. The doorbell resounded with a melodious chime.

After a moment, Frank Monahan answered the door. He stared down at her with his bored expression. "I'm sorry, but Alice isn't at home right now."

"Actually, it's you I'd like to see if you'd be kind enough to give me a bit of your time."

Mr. Monahan worked his lips. "I've got a taxi on order. Catching a flight to L.A. soon for business, but come on in. I've got the orders from the top that I must speak to you if asked."

Guiding Rosa through a tastefully decorated living room, Mr. Monahan led her through a set of sliding glass doors to a spacious wooden patio in a backyard outfitted with comfortable chairs positioned around a frosted-glass patio table. The yard was fenced in by a six-foot-high painted, wooden fence and the lawn was neatly trimmed.

"Please have a seat," Mr. Monahan said. Just then, Diego poked his head out of the satchel. "Holy moly! What's that?"

"I'm so sorry. He won't be a bother. Well, I'm training him not to be, in any case. Is it all right? If not, I can lock him in my car."

Diego let out a soft mew in protest.

Mr. Monahan chuckled. "It's okay with me. Let him roam the yard if you like."

"Fabulous!" Rosa took her host's advice and lifted Diego out of the bag and onto the lawn. He sniffed around him and mewed a couple of times until a rogue butterfly caught his attention. He was off and running.

"Now, what is it that you wanted to see me about?" Mr. Monahan asked.

"Mr. Monahan, I hate to have to mention this, but it's come to my attention that your wife and Mr. Braun may have been...involved."

Mr. Monahan's face flushed an unflattering red. He reached for a package of cigarettes sitting on an end table, removed one, and lit it with a match from a small box beside them. After a long inhale and a slow release of smoke, he said, "My wife became emotionally vulnerable when her sister died. Cancer. Lillian went quickly. The whole family was in shock."

After another drag, he continued, "She and Dieter shared grief that I didn't experience. I couldn't give her the comfort she needed."

"And Mr. Braun did?" Rosa said gently.

"Apparently. I caught them sneaking around. I should've left her then."

"Why didn't you?"

Frank Monahan dropped ashes into the ashtray. "Despite everything, I still love my wife. And if we're honest here, ole man Gainer could make my life very difficult if I crossed him."

Rosa considered his statement. "Where were you last Tuesday evening?"

Frank smiled like he finally had one on her. "I play tennis every Monday and Tuesday night down at the Santa Bonita Tennis club. I played all night both nights."

It was an alibi easily checked, which made for a nice change.

"Who do you think killed Dieter Braun?" Rosa asked.

"Oh, I know this one," Frank said cheekily. "Definitely Walter Gainer."

"Why do you say that?"

"Dieter discovered that Walter was involved in a fire insurance scam at a small tenement building under construction in the Schofield district. Walter had invested heavily in it. A little birdie told me that he was involved in starting a fire. Not personally, of course, but he had a hand in it. He then tried to cash in on the insurance."

Rosa controlled her expression at the shock she felt at Mr. Monahan's accusation. "Arson is a serious crime."

"Hey, if the old man thought it was okay to overturn a few rocks, he can't dictate which ones, right?" A wry grin. "Personally, I think it's time a Gainer went to prison."

Rosa was beginning to think Frank Monahan might just get his way.

"You're saying that Mr. Braun found out about Walter Gainer's illegal activities and then *blackmailed* him?"

"Blackmail is such a dirty word, Miss Reed." Mr. Monahan chortled. "I didn't like Braun, but we were both hitched to the "outsiders" position on the same powerful horse, and that put us on the same side of the game board. I think he relished the thought of having a Gainer over a barrel and was enjoying the fear tactics. Dieter could be vindictive when he wanted to be, all right."

Rosa wrote furiously in her notebook, and then her heart jumped. She'd forgotten about Diego. *Where was the little guy*? Her eyes scanned the lawn, over and under the patio furniture.

"Looking for your cat?" Mr. Monahan said. He pointed, and Rosa followed his gaze.

Diego nonchalantly sunned himself on the top wooden support beam of the fence, licking his paws and washing his face.

Rosa erased the smile that had crept onto her face and returned to the seriousness the matter demanded. "How do you think Dieter found out about the fraud?"

"He told me that Walter Gainer didn't realize that Dieter was part of the group of companies that administered the fire insurance for the building. So, when the fire happened, it was Dieter's fire insurance detective that investigated and found it to be arson. It was easy to put two and two together, but instead of going to the police with it, Dieter kept it secret, wanting to use it as a tool of leverage."

"The police still don't know about the arson?"

"Nobody does except for me, Walter, the insurance detective, and now... you."

15

The office of Braun Insurance was only a few blocks away from Rosa's detective office, and she parked her Corvette in her reserved parking spot next to her building. There was always the chance that Dieter Braun's killer was not part of the Gainer clan, and if that were the case, perhaps a starting point would be at Braun Insurance. If the investigation would eventually take her in that direction, she was more than willing to let the police go after the killer. Her commitment to Orville Gainer ended once the trail left the family.

The receptionist was a pleasing lady with blue eyes tinged with somberness, perhaps due to the recent death of her boss. She wore her brown hair at shoulder length with curls around her ears. The nameplate on her desk read, *Jennifer Schmidt.*

"Hello, I am Rosa Reed. I called earlier to meet with Mr. Tamblyn."

"Oh yes," Miss Schmidt said. "Please have a seat. I'll let him know you're here."

Rosa detected a slight German accent and wondered when the receptionist had immigrated to America. Perhaps she was even a relative of Dieter Braun's.

A minute later, a middle-aged man dressed in a white, long-sleeved shirt, a black tie, and slacks came to greet her. His skin tone was coffee and cream, but his thick curly hair was a mix of black and gray.

The man extended his hand. "Hi, I'm Richard Tamblyn. I understand you wanted to talk to me?"

Rosa stood to shake his hand. "If you don't mind."

Mr. Tamblyn led Rosa into a sparsely furnished office. She sat down on a wooden chair as he gestured towards it.

"I've been engaged by the Gainer family to investigate the death of your now deceased employer, Mr. Braun." Rosa got straight to the point.

He looked a little bit surprised. "Oh? Well now, that is interesting. Do they suspect foul play?"

"I can't really say at this point."

"I will take that as a yes. I know I have an appointment later in the day today with a Detective Belmonte, though they also want to speak to the office manager

Mr. Jennings. You seem to be following a different trail."

Rosa suspected that it would take Detective Belmonte a while longer to track down the lead about the arson. Any information like that would not be forthcoming to him from the Gainers.

"I wanted to ask you about a particular arson investigation."

"Aha. You mean the one involving Walter Gainer."

"Yes, that's the one."

"Mr. Gainer bought fire insurance for a new development out in Schofield. Sounds to me from your accent you're not from around here so you might not be familiar with the area. It's a small town about ten miles northwest of Santa Bonita. We like to call it *North* Santa Bonita though the residents there would object to that. Walter Gainer bought the insurance through a subsidiary company of Dieter Braun's, ironically called *Firesafe Insurance Company*. That company is operated out of an office in Ventura, California. I'm the main investigator for all fire damage claims for that company and several others, including those managed or owned or co-owned by Dieter Braun. Is that why you asked to see me?"

Rosa nodded. "It is."

"Mr. Braun had his fingers in a lot more of the insurance pie than most people realized. Even Walter

Gainer didn't understand that Dieter Braun was involved in *Firesafe Insurance.*"

"In your opinion, the fire in Schofield was arson. Is that correct?"

Mr. Tamblyn's eyebrows raised in appreciation. "You've been doing some digging, Miss Reed. *That's not* common knowledge."

Rosa remained silent, and when the insurance detective saw she wasn't going to reveal her source, he went on. "Usual policy covers gas leaks, structural defects, and so on. However, the fire was most definitely arson. I've got evidence to prove it."

"Thereby nullifying the insurance policy," Rosa said.

"Most likely, though, that part's not up to me. I just investigate the fire itself and stay out of the handling of the claim. Someone else makes the final decisions. I can confirm that someone tried to make it look like a gas leak started the fire. I could go into more details but..."

"No need," Rosa said. She understood his need for confidentiality. She was pleased by what he'd already revealed so far. "What did Mr. Braun do when you showed him your results?"

"He told me to speak to no one. Walter Gainer was his brother-in-law, and he wanted to handle it in-house. That's the last I heard about it." Mr. Tamblyn tapped his pencil on the table. "How well do you know the Gainer family?"

"Just getting to know them. Why do you ask?"

"Orville Gainer is a nasty piece of work, and so are some of his offspring. I wouldn't say this to anyone else, but you seem like a nice lady. I hope you'll be careful. Do you carry a piece?"

The warning stunned her. "A piece?"

"From one detective to another, let me give you some advice." He opened a desk drawer and pulled out a leather shoulder harness with a holster that held a revolver. He pulled out the weapon and put it on the table. "I don't know what they use in England, but here in America, most PIs carry a gun, especially when dealing with shady folks...like the Gainers."

He handled the revolver with fondness as if it were a much-loved baby. "This is my Smith and Wesson .38 Special. The same one the police use. You can order it through the mail."

Rosa stared at Mr. Tamblyn as her mind raced. What had she gotten herself into this time?

Despite Orville Gainer's edict to his family to cooperate with Rosa, Walter Gainer had refused to adjust his schedule to meet her. If she wanted to talk, she'd have to follow him around the "International

Trap Range", which she was happy to do. Having arrived at the shooting range, she made her way toward the figure of Walter Gainer.

Since the first time Rosa had met the eldest Gainer brother, she'd thought he closely resembled his father, but up close the similarities were striking. They shared the same slim build, a firm, square jaw, and an erect posture that suggested a military bearing. Walter's hair, slicked straight back, was styled similarly to Orville Gainer's, although his had not yet turned gray. Today, it was partially covered with a Los Angeles Angels baseball cap. His blue eyes were not as intense as his father's, but when he regarded Rosa, they showed mistrust and irritation.

With only a nod of acknowledgment, he lifted his shotgun and shouted, "Pull!"

A flat, dish-shaped object was catapulted into the air by a fellow operating a small machine. Following the arc of the object for a moment, Walter Gainer fired, which shattered the object into pieces. Rosa opened her mouth to greet him, but he pumped the gun and once again yelled, "Pull!" Another disk was released, but this time the shot missed, and the disk fell to the ground untouched. Walter Gainer cursed under his breath.

With clear reluctance, he turned to Rosa. "I see you found me, Miss Reed." He yelled over to the man operating the machine, "Take a break, Mike. Thanks." He laid the gun across his left arm and motioned for Rosa to sit on a wooden bench.

"Thanks for taking time to speak to me," Rosa said. "I know you have a busy day."

"Yes, well, I didn't have much choice, did I?" He sat down beside her and leaned the gun against the bench.

"I am just trying to get to the bottom of this."

Walter Gainer snorted in derision and shook his head.

"I take it there is some friction between you and your father?"

"That's an understatement. I don't agree with all of this in-house investigation nonsense."

"What do you mean?"

"If, as you say, Dieter was murdered, let's get the police involved. Let's get all the dirty laundry flying in the wind." He rubbed his chin and looked away.

"Dirty laundry?" Rosa probed.

"Yes, my father is especially good at bringing up people's faults and condemning them over and over for it."

Rosa had the feeling she was about to poke a bear. "Are you referring to yourself and your wife?" She remembered what Janet had told her about her sister-in-law's alcoholism.

Walter Gainer snarled. "No doubt Janet has told you all about our troubles. Yes, Patricia has had trouble with the booze in the past, which brought great embarrassment to my father. 'Tarnished the family name.' But she's been on the wagon for years now."

"Tell me about the fire in Schofield."

He turned to her in surprise and then looked away again. He was quiet for a long moment, and Rosa wondered if he would just ignore her. "Well, I'll be damned." He snorted. "You're good at your job; I'll give you that."

"I talked to Richard Tamblyn, the investigator at Dieter Braun's insurance office."

"Of course you did." Walter Gainer shook his head again and fell into another bout of silence.

"I am just following the trails," Rosa said, hoping to prod him along. "It was bound to come out sooner or later. Someone who is owed money on that project will most likely start asking uncomfortable questions soon."

"Heck, I suppose you're right." He grabbed the brim of his baseball cap and slapped it on his thigh in anger. "Have you told anyone?"

"No, but more people in the family know about it than you think. I'm not going to say who, but no one has gone to the police with it."

"The project was going all wrong. Way behind

schedule, disputes with the workers' union, supplies not getting shipped properly...the list goes on."

"So, you decided to cash in on the insurance."

Walter Gainer breathed heavily through his nose. "I was facing bankruptcy and something even worse in this business, a loss of reputation. I have been in the real estate speculation business since the war. I've never had any issues until now. And when Dieter found out, I was at his mercy. He threatened, at least a dozen times, that he was going to go to the police. Then he'd call me an hour later to tell me he was going to wait on it. That he had the keys to my future and that maybe, just maybe, if I was a good boy and paid him handsomely, he would destroy the investigative report and put the rubber stamp on the insurance policy. The man was toying with me." He returned his cap to his head. "Serves me right. Well, I guess I am my father's son, after all."

"What do you mean?"

"Let's just say that the ghosts in the old man's closets are a lot older and more sinister." Walter Gainer grabbed his shotgun and put the butt on his thigh with the barrel pointing up.

"What are you saying, Mr. Gainer?"

"People are dead simply because my father wanted it so." He looked straight at her. "I'd be careful if I were you, Miss Reed. You think you're working for him, but he's playing with you."

Rosa suppressed the shudder that threatened. She didn't doubt Walter Gainer's words and took his warning to heart. Crime families had a way of getting away with murder.

"Do you mind?" she asked, pointing at the gun.

"What...you want to try it?"

"If you'd allow me."

"Well, by all means." He handed her the gun; his mouth turned up in a scornful grin. "This should be entertaining." He then summoned the boy, Mike, who readied himself at the trap thrower. To Rosa, he said, "The gun is a Remington 870 pump-action and holds five rounds in the magazine."

Rosa pumped the gun.

"Careful now," Walter Gainer said. "You follow the pigeon with the barrel and shoot while still in the arc. Breathe steady; there will be quite a kick and—"

Rosa shouted, "Pull!"

The disk flew into the air. Rosa followed it with the barrel and pulled the trigger. A loud boom filled the sky as the disk disintegrated.

"Well, I'll be..." Walter Gainer stared at the sky as if still looking for the disk. "Where d'you learn to shoot like that?"

"Fox hunting is an English pastime, but I prefer

shooting inanimate objects." To Mike, she shouted, "Pull!"

The disk flew again and after another loud boom, was destroyed in an instant.

Rosa pumped the gun again, and the spent cartridge flew onto the ground. "You know what I think?" she said. "I think it could have been a crime of passion. Perhaps you went up to the cabin, hoping to dissuade Dieter Braun. *Pull!*"

The clay disk soared into the air. Rosa squeezed the trigger—hitting the mark, shattering the disk, and watching clay bits fall to the ground.

"There was an argument, and Mr. Braun wouldn't listen to reason." Rosa pumped the shotgun again. "He was working on his Land Rover. You lost your temper and hit him with the claw end of that hammer. Pull!" After the target was once again obliterated, Rosa lowered the gun.

The two stood looking at each other.

"What were you doing last Tuesday night?" Rosa asked, finally.

"Well, Miss Reed, or should I say, Miss Annie Oakley, that is some shooting there. I'm impressed." He nodded appreciatively.

He walked over to take the gun from her hands, but Rosa took one step back, the barrel pointed at the ground, though she knew the magazine was now empty.

"What were you doing last Tuesday night?" she repeated.

"You are a crack shot, Miss Reed, but you missed the target on your little murder theory, I'm afraid. My alibi is weak; I will admit that. I was at home with Patricia. I went to bed around nine thirty after watching our favorite TV show.

Rosa sighed. "Let me guess; *Name That Tune.*"

He looked at her in surprise. "That's right. Are you a fan?"

"I have never seen it, I'm afraid."

"It's an addicting program if you're a music lover. 'Goodnight, Irene' won a young lady forty dollars. Patricia stayed up until eleven reading. Now you can spin your wheels trying to prove I killed Dieter, but if I were you, I would be talking to that Mexican detective. He is closer to solving this than you are—" He held out his hand for the gun. "—by a long shot."

16

The next morning, after a breakfast of waffles and poached eggs, Rosa headed straight for the Santa Bonita Police station. The last thing she wanted to do was see Miguel, especially after that awkward meet up at the restaurant.

However, if there were any truth to what Walter Gainer had told her, she would be wasting her time and effort chasing down the line of investigation that assumed his guilt. It would involve checking out his alibi thoroughly and perhaps finding a way to obtain fingerprints from him to see if they matched any found on the hammer. Or she could try to get him to confess by making him think she had physical evidence or an eyewitness. But before she did that, she needed to find out where the police investigation was at, as uncomfortable as that would be.

Rosa knew the way to Miguel's office and didn't even stop to talk to reception. She found both Miguel and Detective Sanchez standing in front of a large chalkboard that had been wheeled into Miguel's office. They were staring at circles and lines written in chalk with the names of certain Gainer family members. There were also other names, and names of businesses she didn't recognize.

Detective Sanchez, as always, looked like he had just gotten out of bed after having slept in his clothes. He wore the same rumpled white shirt and tie Rosa had seen him wear numerous times. She wondered if the cigarette that perpetually hung from his mouth was the same one she had seen him with weeks ago. Maybe he didn't smoke but left it perched on his mouth unlit because it matched the rest of his ensemble.

He and Miguel both turned to look at her in surprise as she walked in through the opened door.

"Well, come right in, why doncha," Detective Sanchez said, dark eyebrows raised.

"This is a surprise," Miguel remarked. He looked unfairly cool and collected in his summer suit and tie.

"Sorry, gentlemen." Rosa offered a smile, hoping the way Miguel still affected her didn't show on her face. "I was just in the neighborhood."

"Ya, right," Sanchez chuckled. "And we were just about to head to the spa for pedicures." He laughed at his joke and looked at Miguel with a wink. Miguel had a noncommittal smile on his face as if he appreciated the sarcasm but didn't find it as funny as Sanchez did.

Rosa plowed on. "I spoke to Walter Gainer yesterday. He mentioned something that made me think that perhaps we should share some information."

"Well, that's a switch," Miguel said. "Last time I saw you, you seemed pretty determined *not* to collaborate."

"Yes, I'm sorry," Rosa said, feeling remorse about it. "There were, and still are, reasons for that. Perhaps I can explain that to you after the case is solved but for now..." She let out a breath and sat down on a chair. "I want to ask you how you are doing with the investigation of Dieter Braun's murder."

Sanchez and Miguel shared a look. Miguel hesitated and then said, "All right, Rosa, I guess we can trust you. You did direct us to the murder weapon, which we appreciate."

Rosa offered a tight smile.

"How about we tell you," Sanchez started, "and then you tell us what you got." He looked at Miguel, who lifted his chin in agreement.

"Fair enough," Rosa said.

Miguel smiled crookedly. "We got nothing."

Rosa's mouth dropped open. "What?"

"We've gotten nowhere on the case, and Delvecchio is busting our butts about it too. But the Gainer family has shut us out. They aren't telling us anything. Instead, they cover for each other and shut doors in our faces. We have no real leads. We're about to shake that tree again at Dieter Braun's office. Last time we tried, we got nowhere."

Rosa stared at the floor. *Is Walter Gainer trying to throw me off his trail by sending me on a wild goose chase with the police? It seems like a rather weak effort if he is. He must know that one conversation with Miguel would reveal his decoy.* She looked up at the chalkboard. "What is this?"

"This is an older investigation we started on Orville Gainer six months ago in conjunction with a special FBI task force," Miguel said. "We were hoping that it would somehow give up a clue that tied to the murder of Dieter Braun."

Rosa stood and walked to the board. "What kind of investigation?"

"Oh no," Sanchez said, lifting a thick palm. "You give us something first."

Actually, they hadn't *given* her anything, but Rosa played along. "I haven't gotten anywhere either." She stared at the board. Could this old case be what Walter Gainer had been referring to?

"Someone hit Dieter over the head with the claw

end of a hammer," Rosa said to recap, "and then dragged his body into the bomb shelter—"

"And the angle of the wound," Miguel said, cutting in, "the way the shelf fell, the contents strewn about the room, the tobacco, the blood in the vehicle, the spark plug wrench beside the battery—"

Rosa finished. "—Staging the body to make it look like an accident."

"And used the recent earthquake as a cover-up," Miguel said.

"The killer was strong enough to carry a full-grown man down that ladder," Rosa added, "most likely a man."

Miguel nodded. "Agreed. If he were pushed, there would be postmortem lesions."

Rosa tapped on Miguel's desk. "Colin Monahan has a shaky alibi that you can check out if you want. I'll make sure to give you those details before I leave, but in his case, there's no motive that I know of. Other than that, I would take Leo Romano, Frank Monahan, and for the time being, Walter Gainer, off the suspect list. The first two have bulletproof alibis that would be difficult to fake."

Rosa waited a moment while Miguel took notes, then continued. "The family members love the TV show *Name That Tune*. Sidney Gainer and his fiancée were supposedly watching, together with Orville

Gainer. Walter claimed to be watching the same show with his wife, Patricia. They like to think their knowledge of the episode proves their innocence, but it only means they talked to someone who had seen it."

"And?" Miguel prompted.

"They *all* have *motives*, but—"

"But you're not going to tell us what they are," Miguel said.

"You're going to have to trust me," Rosa returned. "Were you able to get fingerprints at the scene?"

"Yes," Sanchez said. "From the ladder, the door handles of the Land Rover and on the shelf—and they weren't Dieter Braun's. They don't match anyone in our records, no surprise there. We also got some prints from the murder weapon."

"Well, that's something," Rosa said hopefully.

"Sure, but the problem is getting fingerprints from any of the Gainers without their consent. None of them have police records. The old trick of bringing them for questioning one by one and getting them to touch a coffee cup probably won't work because, by law, they can have a lawyer present. Any good attorney will be watching like a hawk for stuff like that."

"Okay, here's the scoop." Miguel leaned against the edge of his desk and folded his arms. "We've been investigating Orville Gainer, and certain members of his family, for fraud since February. We think they're involved in a Ponzi scheme."

"It's a type of money fraud," Rosa said, letting the men know she understood.

"It's similar to a pyramid scheme, but with a twist," Sanchez said as he sat in Miguel's office chair and put his feet up on the desk.

"Hey!" Miguel spread his hand out before him in exasperation.

"Oh, sorry." Sanchez took his feet off the desk.

Miguel looked at Rosa and shook his head, "No manners at all. The man is *uncouth*."

"Ooh, nice word," Sanchez quipped.

"Anyway, my rather unrefined partner here is correct," Miguel said, after giving Sanchez another irritated look. "A pyramid scheme is network marketing. Each segment of the pyramid gets a small piece of the money pie while the rest gets forwarded to the top players. The thing collapses when the base of the pyramid gets too big, and not enough people are joining it to sustain it."

Rosa took over from Miguel, "A Ponzi scheme is based on the principle of robbing one person to pay the other. The earlier investors get what was promised them, usually a very high-interest return, but the man in the middle gets more and more money as new investors are enticed by the news that the investment is working as promised. The lure of very high returns is too hard to pass up."

She smiled at the detectives. "My mother met Mr. Ponzi in person when she lived in Boston."

"How intriguing," Miguel said.

"What do these people think they are investing in?" Rosa asked, still staring at the board.

"A real estate investment company called *Saffron Investment Corporation,* which turns out to be an inactive company set up by Orville Gainer, basically a vehicle for various financial maneuvers, especially ones he wants to keep off the radar of the IRS." Miguel pointed to a circle on the chalkboard with the letters '*SIC*' written on it.

"He's telling investors that their money is being used to renovate and build large apartment complexes and commercial buildings in Asia. The explanation for the high returns, usually up to twenty percent in a year, is that building materials and labor costs are much lower, and that buyer interest from the West is huge. There are even one or two construction sites in Thailand, but that represents only a fraction of what has been claimed by SIC.

"In the meantime, we have watched Orville Gainer's assets grow almost exponentially. He has private properties in Barbados, Switzerland, Cabo San Lucas, and even an estate near Panama City, along with several bank accounts in the Cayman Islands. He owns cars, yachts...you name it. But most of it is kept in other countries. He even made a bid to buy into a famous Hollywood studio, but it didn't go through."

Rosa sat back down and considered the implications.

"As I mentioned, we have been monitoring this for almost half a year," Sanchez added. "We always suspected Orville Gainer was the head of this ring along with two, possibly three other main players. Recently, we have come to suspect one of Gainer's grandsons, Sidney Gainer, is involved."

"We nearly have enough evidence to arrest him," Miguel said, "but it's Orville Gainer that we want to bring down. If we arrest Sidney, we're afraid Orville will bolt. With his connections around the globe, well, it would be hard to go after him once he left the country."

Sanchez scratched his chest absentmindedly as he looked at the board. "So, we are biding our time."

"How do you think this Ponzi scheme relates to Dieter Braun?" Rosa asked.

"We haven't figured that part yet," Sanchez said. "It's more or less a hunch."

Miguel pushed off his desk, shooed Sanchez out of his chair, and took his seat. "If Dieter caught on to the scheme, it would give Orville Gainer a big fat motive to kill him."

Rosa felt anger rising in her. "That would mean that Orville Gainer has hired me to solve the murder as a front. He doesn't really think I can solve it. He just likes the appearance of me working on it to throw the police off the trail. After all, why would someone hire a detective to solve a murder if they are involved in the killing?"

No one said anything for a moment, and then with a note of reluctance, Miguel said, "As soon as I found out about the family hiring you, that thought crossed my mind."

"Then why didn't you tell me?"

"You didn't seem exactly eager to talk about it if you recall."

Rosa opened her mouth to reply, but then realized she couldn't, not if she didn't want to risk Miguel's job.

"By the way, why have you come to us now about the murder investigation?" asked Miguel. "Is it because you have been stonewalled by the family too?"

"I interviewed Walter Gainer and, though he didn't give me any details, he did mention that he thought you were closer to solving the murder than I was."

"Well, isn't that sweet of him?" Sanchez scoffed. "We interviewed him a couple days ago, and he gave us absolutely nothing. We even threatened to bring him here for questioning and hold him for twenty-four hours, but he refused to answer one question. He just kept telling us that the Gainer family has the best army of Los Angeles lawyers ever assembled. It was the same line the other Gainers gave us."

"The real question then, is how does he know?" Miguel asked. "How does he know that we are closer?"

Detective Sanchez looked indignant. "Orville Gainer doesn't even know we are investigating him for fraud. How on earth did Walter Gainer find out?"

"Dieter Braun told him," Rosa said, with a sudden revelation.

Miguel caught her eye. "You think so?"

"Yes. After my interview with Walter Gainer, it makes sense."

"We had a feeling it led back to Braun but didn't know how," Miguel said. He tossed a pen onto his desk. "C'mon...let's have it."

"I tell you what," Rosa said, standing. "We can join forces, but I have to keep some things to myself for now. Keep doing what you're doing on this Ponzi scheme investigation, and I'll keep going on the murder investigation. I am convinced now that our paths will cross at some point."

Sanchez and Miguel shared a looked of annoyance.

"Withholding information on a murder investigation carries severe penalties under California law." Miguel eyed Rosa evenly. "I could force you to tell us what you know."

Rosa glanced over her shoulder as she stepped through the open door. "You won't, though."

Miguel scowled.

17

That same afternoon, Rosa sat at her desk and stared at the office phone. It was time to report back to Orville Gainer, and she wanted to collect her thoughts. He had insisted on being informed every step of the way, but now that she knew about the Ponzi scheme investigation, she had to choose her words wisely.

"I was hoping to hear from you today, Miss Reed." Orville Gainer's voice sounded gravelly on the phone. "I've heard that you're doing some digging. Good work. What can you tell me?"

"Leo Romano seems to have a good motive," Rosa said with a tone of somberness, "but his alibi is pretty solid."

"Yes, I knew you would find out about that story about his brother's death in the war, and honestly, I was hoping Leo was the killer. You're sure about his alibi then?"

Rosa cringed at the thought of a man hoping that the father of one of his grandchildren was the killer of his own daughter's husband.

"He and Valerie were on vacation in Florida at the time that earthquake hit last week. Surely you must've known that?" More than ever, Rosa felt like she was merely a toy to be played with, quite like Diego's cloth mouse.

"Oh, yes, of course." Orville chuckled. "I'm getting old, and the gray matter doesn't work like it used to. Anything else?"

"I've interviewed a few others, and I feel I am making good headway. For example, Frank Monahan's alibi seems solid, as well. I'm sure you'll be relieved to hear that your son Walter and grandson Colin Monahan are also not in my immediate sights right now either, for various reasons."

"I agree. I don't suspect either one of them either."

"Sidney also seems to have an alibi."

"Damn right. He was with me on the night of the murder watching TV. He's a good man."

Rosa didn't find comfort in that situation as an alibi for the young Gainer.

"I still have some interviewing to do and more leads to follow," she said. "I'm confident, though, that I will eventually track down the killer. These things usually take time. It's only been a few days."

Rosa wanted to sound upbeat, at least for now. The next time she reported to him, she would feign sounding frustrated. There could be a point where he would simply ask her to give up the chase and admit defeat. Especially when he suspected that she was getting close.

"I'm sure you'll solve this whole wretched thing in good time, Miss Reed. From what I can tell, we have managed to shut out the police completely. Keep up the good work!"

Through the praise, Rosa detected the scorn in his voice.

They said their goodbyes, and Rosa hung up the phone. A knock at her office front door claimed her attention, and she found a young man on the other side, dressed in a United Parcel Service uniform and holding a medium-sized box. "Special Expedited Delivery for Miss Rosa Reed."

Rosa signed for the parcel, took it back to her desk, and opened it to reveal a slightly smaller metal box with the words "*Smith and Wesson*" inscribed on it. Four smaller, green-colored cardboard boxes with "*Remington*" printed on the label were included. The delivery had come sooner than expected, but then it was only less than a day's drive to Burbank, California, where the Smith and Wesson distributorship was located.

Opening the metal box, she lifted out the brand-new Smith and Wesson Colt Cobra—a .38 Special revolver with a two-inch barrel—and slipped it out of the oilskin cloth. She felt the well-balanced weight of the gun, eyed the shiny blue finish, and admired the checkered walnut handgrip. She stared down the short barrel with her arm straight out in front of her and pointed at the lamp.

Walter Gainer had called her *Annie Oakley*. Rosa had gone to see *Annie Get Your Gun,* the famous American musical comedy, with her parents in London when it had come to the cinema five years earlier. The actress Betty Hutton had received a Golden Globe nomination for best actress, and Rosa felt the award had been well-deserved.

However, this was no musical nor a comedy. But this "Annie" had gotten her gun, and like the original western sharpshooter, she had a steady hand and a sharp eye. She wasn't afraid of anyone, including rich tyrants and their unsavory offspring.

Rosa met Miguel and Detective Sanchez on a bench overlooking Santa Bonita pier. Down below, was Sidney Gainer's yacht, *The Conqueror*. All three wore sunglasses and sipped creamy milkshakes purchased from an ice cream shop just steps from the public bench where they sat—Detective Sanchez in the middle. For a few minutes, no one spoke, and the only sound was occasional slurping and the stirring of melting ice cream with the paper-made *flex* straws.

Like three kids hanging out after school, Rosa thought.

"Gee whiz, I wish I could afford a boat like that," Sanchez mused.

"Not me." Miguel lifted the bottom end of the straw into his mouth and used it as a small spoon to get a chunk of ice cream. "I prefer my feet firmly on the ground."

Rosa glanced at Miguel as a memory flashed before her from over a decade before. She and Miguel, in the throes of their romance, had taken out a rowboat in this very bay. A larger boat had carelessly gone past them, creating big waves, and in moments, the rowboat had tipped over.

It was when Rosa had learned that Miguel couldn't swim.

She'd saved his life.

He'd professed his love.

And now, with the way Miguel had leaned forward and stared hard at her, she could tell he remembered too.

They broke their locked gazes simultaneously and vigorously sipped on their milkshakes.

Detective Sanchez remained unaware of the emotional quake that had just happened. "Say, I bet Larry Rayburn owns a boat."

Miguel kept his sights on the ocean, deftly refusing to look at Rosa again. Detective Sanchez knew Rosa's connection to the assistant medical examiner, but like Larry, didn't know about the history she and Miguel had once shared.

Rosa sighed, lifted her glass to her mouth, and swallowed the last of her drink. She then tipped the large glass on its side on the bench beside her. Diego poked his head out of the satchel–red and white striped fabric, this time, to match Rosa's summer dress —and immediately licked the remnants of the ice cream on the side of the glass.

After a long beat, Miguel said, "Why do you say that about Rayburn?"

Detective Sanchez shrugged a thick shoulder. "I heard he's from Galveston. I heard sailing's a big deal there."

Rosa confirmed the story. "He is. He was raised on the ocean."

"You would know," Miguel muttered then slid Rosa a sideways glance that appeared apologetic. He was being unprofessional, and they both knew it.

Detective Sanchez pointed to *The Conqueror.* "Hey, look, there he is."

The three watched as Sidney Gainer climbed out of his boat, stepped onto the pier, and turned to help a shapely brunette who wore a white bikini, step out of the boat. Detective Sanchez grabbed the binoculars beside him and adjusted them to focus. "Ooh la la, that is some *naughty* bathing attire!"

"May I?" Rosa said, holding out a palm. She received the binoculars from Detective Sanchez and adjusted the lenses. "Hmm, now isn't that interesting. That is definitely *not* his fiancée." She followed the couple as they walked hand in hand along the pier to the shore and disappeared behind a block of apartments. "I bet he picked her up in San Diego."

"I wonder what this means?" Miguel said.

"It *means* his ties to his fiancée might be negligible at best," Rosa replied. "That's good for us because, gentlemen, it means the chances of our little plan working have just improved."

18

A short time later, Rosa parked right in front of Sidney Gainer's grand house. Stepping through the gate, she walked with purpose down the long tiled walkway, then into the shaded alcove at the front door, and rang the bell.

Rosa had expected a maid or butler to open the massive oak door, but it was Sidney Gainer himself who stood with a mild look of surprise on his attractive face. "Well, this is unexpected," he said. "Please, come in."

He directed Rosa to the back of the house and onto a large wooden deck overlooking a small beach down below. The place offered a spectacular view of the ocean. Rosa took the proffered seat.

"It's always a pleasure to entertain an attractive

lady in my humble home," he gestured around him with a look of pride.

"It certainly is a lovely view you have here," Rosa said. "And it's such a warm day. Do you think I could trouble you for a glass of water? I'm rather parched."

"Of course." Sidney Gainer disappeared for a moment and came back with a small glass of iced water. Wearing short white gloves, Rosa accepted the glass and took a large gulp.

"To what do I owe this nice surprise? Wait, you're surely not going to tell me that you have found proof that I knocked off my uncle Dieter, are you?" He smiled and made a slight chopping motion with his right hand as if he were holding a hammer.

Rosa's blood ran cold. *So sure of himself*, she thought.

"Well, not just yet," she said without a hint of humor. "These things take time, you know."

Sidney blinked rapidly as his confident smirk slowly faded.

Rosa offered a comforting smile. "Actually, you're not really on the radar screen, at the moment. I mean, certainly your alibi—watching television with your grandfather and your fiancée—would be a hard one to crack."

A look of relief flashed behind Sidney's eyes.

"Speaking of your fiancée," Rosa continued. "Debbie's not here, is she?"

"No. I'm afraid she's out of town."

"Is she? Oh well, I would love to talk to her sometime."

"Yeah, well, she isn't here, so—"

"You're alone, then?"

For a split second, Sidney's eyes darted over Rosa's shoulder into the house. Rosa made a show of turning around to follow his gaze. She then stared at him with one eyebrow raised. His expression suddenly lost all congeniality.

"What do you want, Miss Reed?" he said with a note of irritation.

"Does the family know?"

"Know what?"

"About your affair. A pretty brunette, am I right?"

"Have you been spying on me?"

Rosa grinned at the man's nerve to sound incredulous.

"I've been hired by your grandfather to do whatever I have to do to track Mr. Braun's killer. You are aware that you're required to cooperate."

"Fine. What is it that you *want*?"

"Relax, Mr. Gainer. I am investigating a murder. I'm quite uninterested in what you do in your private life unless it's toppling over shelves in bomb shelters."

Sidney snorted.

"Or going on late night walks out on the cabin pier."

He wouldn't have known that the police had found the hammer. His eyes narrowed. "I have no idea what you're talking about. Get to the point, *please*."

"You told me the other day about your dream of sailing your yacht around the world."

"Yeah, so,"

"If I were you, I would get started on that right away."

"What?"

"You must have somewhere you want to go. With all the money you made from...what is it called now? Saffron or something? You know, those interesting investments you've been involved with overseas."

Sidney glared. "How do you know about that?" His fingers formed tight fists and loosened again. "It doesn't matter, anyway. Those are legitimate business interests."

"Yes. Very high returns from what I hear."

"Which is what makes it a good investment."

"Of course. Out of respect to your grandfather, I thought I should warn you that the police are tossing around the word *Ponzi* concerning you."

Sidney's face went as white as the hull of a new boat bobbing on the bay.

"Why me?" he muttered.

Rosa shrugged. "I suppose the police have to pin it on someone, and your grandfather is too powerful. You must know that the FBI is involved, and should you be arrested, you could be looking at twenty years."

Sidney Gainer's fingers flicked in and out of tight fists as his neck grew red with emotion.

Fear? Anger?

Rosa pushed the final button. With soft eyes, she leaned forward and touched his arm. "*You* just seem like a good man, Mr. Gainer, simply caught up in the wrong thing at the wrong time. Personally, I admire your courage and innovation. I just wanted to warn you, in case..."

Rosa stood to leave. "I hear the weather in South America is very nice right now." When Sidney shifted in his seat, she held out a palm. "Please, don't trouble yourself. I can find my way out."

After she had met with Sidney Gainer, Rosa once again joined Miguel, who had returned to their spot on the bench overlooking the pier. His unmarked cruiser, parked a few feet away, had the windows down, and Rosa could just hear the chatter on the police radio. Dark clouds on the horizon moved in rather ominously, though the bay remained calm.

Without greeting her, Miguel said, "Sanchez got clearance from the chief to commandeer a police boat and will be watching from a safe distance with the two-man crew. He hasn't let me know he's in place, but I expect he will soon." He cupped his eyes with one hand as he searched the horizon. "According to the forecast, the weather's not going to be our friend today. If we're lucky, we can get this done before the storm hits." Miguel eyed Rosa's satchel. "Did you get it?"

Rosa produced a forensic bag wrapped in protective padded cloth. Inside the bag was a small drinking glass.

Miguel's expression cheered. "Bingo!" He walked the bagged drinking glass to his unmarked car and placed it in a metal evidence container. They just had to wait for lab results to show if Sidney Gainer's prints matched the ones found at Dieter Braun's bomb shelter and on the murder weapon.

Rosa picked up the binoculars Miguel had left on the bench and focused on the yacht. The plan was simple, but if all went well, would lead to a break in at least one of the two investigations. It would be highly incriminating if Sidney Gainer were caught fleeing the country with suitcases and a passport in hand, especially after having just learned about the Ponzi investigation. And, after a short but dramatic police boat chase, it could even lead to a confession of the fraud. It would also prove a motive for killing Dieter Braun if Walter Gainer testified in court about Dieter Braun's knowledge of the Ponzi scheme.

"Oh," Rosa said, as their mark came into her frame. "He's here already, and he's got a suitcase. No girlfriend, though. He must have ditched her or something. He seems in a hurry." She handed the binoculars to Miguel.

"Sanchez isn't in place yet," Miguel said.

Rosa shot him a look. "If we wait, we could miss him."

"I know," Miguel agreed.

Rosa jumped to her feet. "Ahoy, Detective Belmonte! It's time for a boat ride. Let's execute the stowaway plan."

Miguel's eyes went wide. "*You* know I can't swim. I have a strong boat phobia!"

In a flash to the past, Rosa was swimming through cold water, fighting the wake from a negligent yacht and the subsequent undercurrent. Her lungs burned from holding her breath, and her legs felt like noodles. She'd have given up, let herself float, trusting she'd eventually make it to shore except that Miguel's dark head had disappeared under the water.

Fear, at that moment, had gripped her. In desperation, she'd fought against nature as if she were fighting for her own life.

She'd never forget the horror she'd felt in those eternal moments when she couldn't find him.

Then she had had his shirt in her fingers, and with supernatural strength, she heaved his heavy form out of the water and onto the tipped-over rowboat. *Miguel!*

Slamming his back with her fist, she'd forced water out of his lungs, then putting her lips over his, breathed life back into him.

"Rosa!"

Rosa snapped back to reality. Miguel, faced with the prospect of jumping onto another boat, looked close to panic, his jaw tight with emotion.

"It's okay, Miguel," she said. "I can go by myself."

She ran down the path to the pier; her purse secured diagonally over her shoulder to her hip.

"Damn it!" Miguel said.

Rosa heard his footsteps right behind her.

As the pair reached the bottom of the pathway, they saw Sidney Gainer untether the docking ropes, climb onto the roof of his yacht, and enter the canopied flybridge.

Rosa and Miguel quickened their pace again as the twin engines sprang to life with a rumble. Sidney jotted in a notebook. This pause gave them time to jump across the gap between the pier and the boat. They landed with a soft thud, instinctively ducking down. Rosa glanced up as Sidney squinted in their direction. She tugged on Miguel's shirt, pulling him to the floor behind a large white, vinyl-covered engine hood. Her heart pounded. *Had they been spotted?*

Miguel risked a second look. "He didn't see us."

Where was Sanchez? He was supposed to be ready to give chase. Either way, she and Miguel couldn't stay crouched in their hiding spot forever. Once they had traveled far enough to prove that Sidney Gainer was on the run and not just out for a cruise in the harbor, they must confront him.

Miguel squatted low beside Rosa, his face was a lighter shade of olive than its usual tone, but he gave her a thumbs up and a nervous half-smile.

Just as the engine rose in pitch and the boat moved away from the slip, Rosa poked her head up over the engine cowl.

Por todos los santos!

They weren't the only stowaways. Just as the yacht pulled away from the dock, Colin Monahan slipped aboard. Carrying a suitcase, he crouched low and made his way to the door of the lower cabin, then disappeared inside.

The yacht cleared the dock area and accelerated.

Rosa's mind raced. What was Colin Monahan doing on the boat? And why would he *sneak* onboard? She flashed back to the conversation she'd had with him in the roadside café. *I have proven that no matter what I do, I can't please the old man...*

Was he here to prove himself in some way? Had Orville Gainer discovered that Sidney was about to run and sent Colin Monahan to stop him?

The questions rattled through Rosa's head, and then, like a marble thrown into a funnel, she came to one terrifying possibility: *Colin Monahan killed Dieter Braun and was here to kill his cousin!*

It suddenly made sense. It wasn't Sidney Gainer's fingerprints they would find on that hammer; it would be Colin Monahan's. The young man with an unpredictable temper. The grandson who could never please his grandfather. Perhaps he had made a bid to win his favor by killing Dieter Braun, the man who could damage the elder Gainer. When that hadn't garnered the results he'd hoped for, he'd decided to harm the favored grandson. And what better place to do it than on a yacht heading out to sea.

"We both learned to sail together on my grandfather's luxury yacht. We would often go out on excursions together as teenagers."

Extreme, lifelong jealousy made for a compelling motive. Did Colin Monahan plan to murder his cousin, throw the body overboard, and continue to anywhere in the world? It would explain the suitcase. He could even take on his dead cousin's stolen identity.

Rosa turned once again to look at Miguel, sitting with his back leaning against the engine compartment with eyes closed, sweat pouring off his forehead. His lips moved as if he were quietly and desperately praying. She slapped him hard on the thigh.

"Miguel!"

Miguel's eyelids flickered open.

Rosa leaned in to speak in his ear, but the roar of the engines was loud, and she had to shout to be heard. "Colin Monahan has just come onboard. I think he might be the killer!"

Miguel looked at her with a wild expression of bewilderment. She rose once again to look toward the lower cabin door as Miguel poked his head around the engine cowl. As predicted, the weather had turned, and the waves conspired against the boat. The water got much rougher, causing the boat to buck violently. The dark clouds released a sudden batch of heavy rain. They were now clear of the bay and speeding along on a southerly route about a mile from shore.

Where was Sanchez?

Suddenly, Colin Monahan appeared in the doorway of the lower cabin, and Rosa and Miguel quickly ducked behind the engine cowl. Peeking from her hiding place, Rosa saw Colin grab the ladder railing that led to the flybridge, gun in hand.

19

A large rolling wave hit the side of the vessel, throwing Rosa and Miguel through the air. Rosa expected to hit the hard, slippery deck but instead felt Miguel's warm body underneath her. When she lifted her head, she stared into his startled copper-brown eyes, and everything around her froze in time. The boat stopped bobbing, the sea spray and rain-drops froze in midair. Rosa hadn't been this close to Miguel since she was seventeen.

Miguel gasped, and then deftly rolled to one side. It was as if an invisible hand switched the rain and wind on again, and Rosa grabbed the rail and hoisted herself to her feet, catching her breathing. Miguel did the same and then focused on the sight of Colin Monahan as he worked his way up the ladder to the flybridge. Colin struggled against the rocking of the boat and the stiff rain, using his one free hand and the elbow of the other arm to pull himself up.

Miguel and Rosa lurched toward the ladder. Just as Colin stepped out of sight, Miguel started up with Rosa right behind. When Miguel reached the top, he released his police revolver from his holster and yelled, "Put it down!"

At the same moment, the engines suddenly cut and the boat slowed dramatically. Reaching the flybridge, Rosa braced herself against the closest rail. Miguel stood on the other side of the ladder, one white-knuckled fist gripping a side rail and the other pointing his revolver.

Colin Monahan stood behind Sidney with his gun to his cousin's temple. Sidney, whose wrists were bound, sat in the captain's chair. He stared at Rosa and Miguel with glassy-eyed fear. The slightest jolt of the yacht could end his life in an instant.

Seeing Miguel with his gun raised, Colin's eyes went wide open.

"Colin," Rosa said, forcing herself to remain calm. "Put the gun down."

The boat slowed but continued to pitch and roll. They now had cover from the rain. Rosa glanced at Miguel, whose face had drained of color. She instinctively moved toward him.

"Don't take another step!" Colin Monahan shouted.

Rosa froze in her spot.

He shouted again, "Wh... what are you two doing on board?"

"It's all right, Colin," Rosa said, gesturing with a downward motion with her hands. "Let's talk." She glanced at Miguel, who had turned a distressing shade of green and looked like he could be sick at any moment.

The floor beneath them all rolled violently, and help was not in sight. Rosa needed to get Colin talking, and better yet, get him to drop the gun.

Colin's desperation carried as he shouted, "How did you two suddenly just appear?"

"We were following Sidney," Rosa returned. "We suspected that he was going to make a run for it. The question, Colin, is why are you here? Did you come here to *kill* your cousin?"

Colin looked astounded by the accusation. "*No.* I came here to *steal* the boat. I didn't know this scum was going to beat me to the punch."

Rosa's gaze fell to Sidney, who'd curled into himself in fear. "Do you mean this boat belongs to someone else?"

"Of course," Colin said. "It belongs to the old man, like everything and everyone else in Santa Bonita. But

Sidney and I own some property in Panama, don't we?" He tightened his grip on Sidney Gainer's shoulder, causing his captive to wince. "That's where you were heading, weren't you, *cousin*?"

"I... I tried to get a hold of you," Sidney sputtered. "I wanted you to come with me."

Rosa didn't believe that for a second, and apparently, neither did Colin.

"Don't lie to me, Sid! You're always lying to me!"

As if he could dodge the nose of the gun, Sidney's head bent to the side, but Colin kept it tightly against Sidney's temple.

"You didn't plan to kill your Uncle Dieter did you, Colin," Rosa said quickly, keeping her voice smooth and reasonable. "I know you feel angry, but killing isn't your thing."

It was a gamble. Rosa didn't know for sure who had killed Dieter Braun, but Colin's face flushed with surprise at her statement of belief in him.

"Colin, please put down the gun."

Colin snorted. "You underestimate me, Miss Reed, but that seems to happen a lot around here. Maybe killing *is* my thing."

Tears rolled down his ruddy face, and Rosa felt a stab of pity for the boy who felt he could do nothing right.

"Talk to me," Rosa said. "How did it happen?"

With each question she posed, she took a small step toward Miguel.

Colin ducked his chin toward Sidney. "I know Grandpa had ordered this piece of *crap* to kill Uncle Dieter. Dieter found out about that stupid real estate scam and kept threatening to blow the whistle. I told him to stop, but he wouldn't *listen*! Uncle Dieter always treated me okay, but damn he was stubborn! *Why was he so stubborn?*" He shouted out the last sentence to the sky.

Rosa moved slowly to Miguel's side.

"You didn't go up to the cabin to kill him, though," Rosa said.

"I tried to talk to him. I tried...I really tried. I told him refusing to listen to reason would be dangerous. He just laughed. He laughed *hard.* I couldn't take that, him laughing so hard...everyone laughs at me. The old man laughs at me."

"And afterward," Rosa said, finishing for him, "when you realized what you'd done, you carried him to the bomb shelter."

Colin cried openly now, tears streaming like the rain falling around them. "Yes, and when I told Grandpa that he didn't have to worry, that his precious *Sidney* didn't have to risk jail after all—"

Miguel finished the sentence this time, "—he was angry."

"He shouted at me and told me to get out!"

Rosa worried that Colin might shoot Sidney without meaning to, but instead, his arm went limp. Weeping, he dropped the gun, which hit the floor with a clang and slid off the flybridge to the deck below. Rosa then removed her gun from her purse, pointed it at Colin, and gestured to Miguel, who regarded her gun with surprise. Miguel holstered his weapon and took out his handcuffs.

Colin smiled at Rosa. Then in one dreadful moment, she knew what he was going to do.

"Colin, don't!"

Before the words were out of her mouth, Colin catapulted himself over the rail. Rosa reached it just in time to see him hit the waves and disappear under the angry white caps.

In the distance, a police boat raced toward them.

20

Thirty people stood around the grave of Dieter Braun as the casket was slowly lowered into the dark earth. The morning was unusually crisp, even at 10:00 a.m., and Rosa fought off a chill as she stood beside a tearful Janet Gainer. Her husband, Michael, stood beside her, hands clasped at his waist and a somber expression on his face. Janet had been chosen to give the eulogy, probably as one of the few family members inclined to say something nice about the deceased. Rosa thought she had done a wonderful job.

Mr. Braun's business associates, his friends outside the family, and the Gainer clan, except for Colin Monahan, were present. Colin's attempt at escaping justice by jumping off the yacht had been thwarted by Detective Sanchez's timely arrival with the police boat, and Colin's instinctive impulse to breathe. Unlike Miguel, Colin Monahan knew how to swim.

Sidney Gainer, his face impassive with his eyes hidden by sunglasses, stood next to his fiancée, Debbie, but neither seemed to take comfort in the other. Rosa predicted that the wedding was unlikely to take place—quite possibly, Sidney would spend some time in prison—and future family reunions would prove very awkward for the cousins.

In a show of moral support, Walter and Patricia Gainer stood next to Orville Gainer, flanked by the two police officers assigned to escort him while on house arrest. Being friendly with the judge clearly had its advantages. Dressed in a black suit and black fedora hat, the elder Gainer showed no signs of remorse on his lined face. His pale-blue eyes appeared cold and calculating as the casket chains finally went slack, and the casket touched ground at the bottom of the hole.

The service ended, and the crowd began a slow retreat. Janet stepped in beside Rosa.

"I regret hiring you," she said. "I only wanted to find my brother-in-law. Had I known about Colin—"

And her son, Sidney, Rosa thought. She said, "I'm sorry."

"It's not your fault, Miss Reed."

Miss Reed. Janet had firmly placed her out of her friendship circle.

"But family is family," Janet continued. "We have the best lawyers money can buy. If there's a loophole, we'll find it." She lowered her voice. "If not, we'll make one."

Rosa shivered. She sincerely hoped that Janet Gainer's threats were empty. Either way, there would be more arrests. She wondered how much Janet knew about the Ponzi scheme?

"Once again," Rosa said kindly. "I'm sorry for your loss."

Turning away, Rosa slowly walked to her car. To her surprise, Miguel, dressed in a dark suit and sunglasses leaned against it. As she approached, he took off his sunglasses, tucked them into his shirt pocket, and straightened.

"That's right, Detective Belmonte," Rosa said with a hint of a smile. "You'd better not let me catch you leaning against my Corvette."

Miguel smiled, pulled out a handkerchief, and made a mock gesture of dusting off a spot on the car's fender. But when Rosa reached him and leaned on the fender, Miguel resumed his spot. They stared ahead, watching the funeral attendees. Most were still chatting while some drifted back to their cars.

"I wouldn't have gotten on that boat, if not for you," Miguel finally remarked.

Rosa hummed.

"I start lessons in two weeks."

Rosa crossed her arms. "Good to hear it."

Miguel lifted his chin. "I get to save your life next time."

"Be my guest." A smile tugged at one corner of Rosa's mouth.

"Probably won't be in water, but maybe some other way."

"I am sure it will be very heroic," she offered.

There was a long silence.

"Nice gun," Miguel said.

"Glad you like it. It has a two-inch barrel."

"I noticed that. That's pretty neat."

"Thank you."

Another long silence.

"Rosa, I…"

"How is the Ponzi case coming along?" Rosa somehow knew Miguel wanted to talk about Charlene Winters and Larry Rayburn, but didn't want to have a conversation right now. She could easily read him because he wasn't the type to hide his feelings. It was one of the things that had first drawn her to him all those years ago. Things had been complicated then, and they were complicated now. Suddenly, Rosa desperately found herself wanting an uncomplicated life, and that meant trying to keep an emotional distance from Miguel Belmonte.

"Um, it's going okay." Miguel put on his sunglasses again. He seemed to understand. "Sanchez and I spoke to Walter Gainer yesterday. He's willing to testify in court about what he learned from Dieter Braun."

Rosa wondered if Walter Gainer would go through with it. After what Janet had said about the family, Rosa wouldn't be surprised if they circled the wagons.

"We also now have FBI documents in our possession showing funds were being transferred from prospective *Saffron* investors directly to Orville Gainer via offshore accounts. I have testimony from Dieter's associate in Los Angeles, Melvyn Freeman, the one who originally told Dieter about the Ponzi scheme." Miguel took a small step back. "We are almost ready to make arrests. In the meantime, Orville Gainer is under house arrest and Sidney Gainer is under close police surveillance. No one is going to leave town. Old man Gainer doesn't know everything we have on him, but he certainly knows some of it, as does Sidney Gainer. They must be sweating in their boots right now. We'll get them."

Miguel paused and shifted his weight as he crossed his arms and looked at Rosa. "There is one thing I don't understand; why did you withhold certain information from me in the beginning? It's not like you, and I don't believe it's because you wanted the credit of solving the murder on your own."

Rosa sighed. "Orville Gainer threatened to have you kicked out of the force if you got too close." She glanced up, unsure how he'd react to that news. "He says he still has a lot of leverage with someone high up in the police administration. Orville Gainer doesn't strike me as the kind of person who makes a threat unless he thinks he can carry it out."

Miguel had his sunglasses on, so Rosa couldn't see his eyes, but the way his jaw muscle protruded told her he was staring at her with smoldering anger.

"I don't need you to protect me, Rosa."

"I know."

He dropped his arms and stepped in front of her. "Do you? You put yourself in unnecessary danger! What if something had happened to you because of me? Do you think I could live with that?"

Rosa swallowed. She hadn't seen this kind of intense emotion from Miguel since the day she'd boarded the plane for London back in 1945.

"I'm sorry, Miguel."

Miguel let out a long, hard breath. "Just promise me you won't do it again, okay? I can look after myself."

He turned his back to her and stormed away.

Without feeling a thread of regret, Rosa slid into her Corvette. She'd always protect Miguel Belmonte, and she knew he'd always protect her. They might not be a couple anymore, but they were *something*.

Rosa put the Corvette into drive and headed north on the wide coastal highway, the wind in her hair and the radio on.

Murder's a wrap!

Private Investigator Rosa Reed has finally accepted that her girlhood romance with Detective Miguel Belmonte has no hope of being rekindled, but when his actress girlfriend gets embroiled in a murder on her movie set, it's more than a movie schedule that's upsetting. Can Rosa put aside matters of the heart long enough to help Miguel solve the case?

Find it on AMAZON

Did you read the PREQUEL?

Rosa & Miguel's Wartime Romance is a BONUS short story exclusively for Lee's newsletter subscribers.

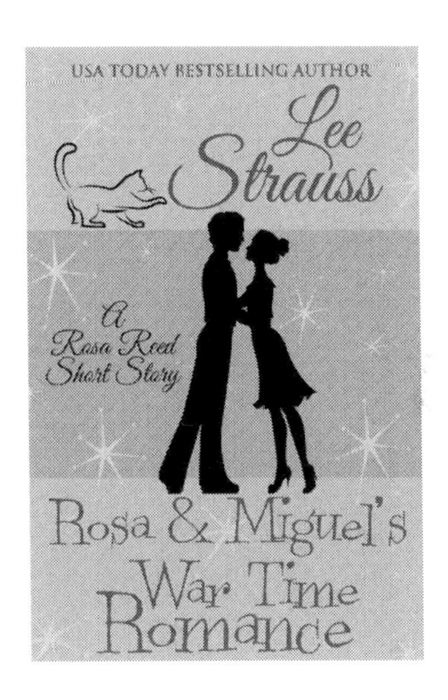

How it All Began. . .

Like many British children during World War Two, Rosa Reed's parents, Ginger and Basil Reed, made the heart-wrenching decision to send their child to a foreign land and out of harm's way. Fortunately, Ginger's half-sister Louisa and her family, now settled in the quaint coastal town of Santa Bonita, California, were pleased to take her in.

By the spring of 1945, Rosa Reed had almost made it through American High School unscathed, until the American army decided to station a base there. Until she met the handsome Private Miguel Belmonte and fell in love. . .

READ FREE!

Don't miss the latest Ginger Gold Mystery!
MURDER AT BRIGHTON BEACH
Book 13

Murder's a Beach!

A family holiday turns deadly at Brighton Beach. When Ginger and Basil and their family check into the

Grand Brighton Hotel on a lovely warm day in June of 1926, a shocking discovery upsets their plans to relax in the sun and surf.

Not only will Ginger not finish her book, she and Basil might not get out alive.

Find it on AMAZON

Start from the beginning ~ Murder on the SS Rosa!

Find it on AMAZON

Also on audio!

ROSA & MIGUEL'S WARTIME ROMANCE

PREQUEL - EXCERPT

Rosa Reed first laid eyes on Miguel Belmonte on the fourteenth day of February in 1945. She was a senior attending a high school dance, and he a soldier who played in the band.

She'd been dancing with her date, Tom Hawkins, a short, stalky boy with pink skin and an outbreak of acne, but her gaze continued to latch onto the bronze-skinned singer, with dark crew-cut hair, looking very dapper in a black suit.

In a life-changing moment, their eyes locked. Despite the fact that she stared at the singer over the shoulder of her date, she couldn't help the bolt of electricity that shot through her, and when the singer smiled—and those dimples appeared—heavens, her knees almost gave out!

"Rosa?"

Tom's worried voice brought her back to reality. "Are you okay? You went a little limp there. Do you feel faint? It is mighty hot in here." Tom released Rosa's hand to tug at his tie. "Do you want to get some air?"

Rosa felt a surge of alarm. Invitations to step outside the gymnasium were often euphemisms to get fresh.

In desperation she searched for her best friend Nancy Davidson—her best *American* friend, that was. Vivien Eveleigh claimed the position of *best* friend back in London, and Rosa missed her. Nancy made for a sufficient substitute. A pretty girl with honey-blond hair, Nancy, fortunately, was no longer dancing, and was sitting alone.

"I think I'll visit the ladies, Tom, if you don't mind."

He looked momentarily put out, then shrugged. "Suit yourself." He joined a group of lads—boys—at the punch table, and joined in with their raucous laughter. Rosa didn't want to know what they were joking about, or at whose expense.

Nancy understood Rosa's plight as she wasn't entirely pleased with her fellow either. "If only you and I could dance with each other."

"One can't very well go to a dance without a date, though," Rosa said.

Nancy laughed. "*One* can't."

Rosa rolled her eyes. Even after four years of living in America, her Englishness still manifested when she was distracted.

And tonight's distraction was the attractive lead singer in the band, and shockingly, he seemed to have sought her face out too.

Nancy had seen the exchange and gave Rosa a firm nudge. "No way, José. I know he's cute, but he's from the wrong side of the tracks. Your aunt would have a conniption."

Nancy wasn't wrong about that. Aunt Louisa had very high standards, as one who was lady of Forrester mansion, might.

"I'm only looking!"

Nancy harrumphed. "As long as it stays that way."

Continue reading >>>

Rosa & Miguel's Wartime Romance is a BONUS short story exclusively for Lee's newsletter subscribers.

Subscribe Now!

SNEAK PEEK - MURDER ON LOCATION

One of the first things that attracted Rosa Reed to Dr. Larry Rayburn, assistant medical examiner for the Santa Bonita Police Department, had been that he was the picture of Texas charm. As a former Woman Police Constable for the London Metropolitan Police, Rosa had worked with many pathologists and found most capable and efficient, but they were a little, well, "stiff". Perhaps that came with the job of examining corpses all day. Larry Rayburn, however, defied any stereotypes Rosa had ever had. As a Londoner, she appreciated his gentle formality—but just below that was a funny, unpretentious, and kind man that Rosa enjoyed.

Still, she had to occasionally stifle a giggle when he came to pick her up for a date. He drove a 1948 faded-green Chevrolet pickup truck with its heavy rounded hood, large bug-eyed headlights, and painted grille.

Larry had regaled Rosa with stories about how he used to drive the machine on his father's ranch in Galveston, and though he kept saying he meant to trade it in for "a nicer chariot", Rosa suspected her date was a little more attached to the truck than he liked to let on. So tonight, as she watched him trundle into the elegant and expansive Forrester estate in his faithful mechanical steed, she grinned at the incongruous sight.

The Forrester mansion was a sprawling Spanish-style structure, built on a low hill overlooking the Pacific Ocean, and was a testament to her late Uncle Harold's wealth and his success as an oil baron. It boasted many acres of land, manicured gardens, a swimming pool, and a tennis court. The long driveway was lined with swaying palm trees and ended in a circle surrounding an angel-pouring-water fountain.

Not bothering to wait for Larry to come to the door —and saving him from another embarrassing interrogation by her Aunt Louisa who, in Rosa's opinion, was overly enthusiastic about her budding relationship— Rosa stepped out into the warm and breezy California sunshine.

Already out of the truck and opening the passenger door, Larry tipped his straw fedora, winked with his deep-blue eyes twinkling, and said, "Hiya, Miss Reed."

"Hello, Dr. Rayburn," she teased as they were on a first-name basis. Rosa, shifting the crinolines of her black-and-white checkered skirt—embossed with red cherries that matched her red form-fitting, fine-knit sweater—kissed Larry before she climbed into his truck. Gloria, her younger and society-minded cousin, had been with Rosa when they were lingerie shopping and had encouraged the purchase of a bullet brassiere, named such for its rather pointy design. Rosa felt a tad self-conscious wearing it, but Larry, if one could go by his cheeky grin, seemed quite taken with her outfit.

Along with her white half-hat angled on her head of short chestnut curls, short white gloves, and black ballet shoes, Rosa was appropriately dressed for going to the movies and was looking forward to the evening.

Showing at the Santa Bonita Cinema was an action flick called *The Last Clue* starring Nicholas Post. Though Rosa had only recently heard of the star, Gloria had told her, most emphatically, that in America, he was as famous as Cary Grant or Humphrey Bogart.

"You should like this one," Larry said as they moseyed along the main road. "Nicholas Post plays a hard-boiled private investigator."

"I'd hardly call myself hard-boiled." Rosa had recently set up Reed Investigations in Santa Bonita, and though she worked as a private investigator, she didn't think she could be compared to the character in this film.

Larry chuckled and took her hand. "No, darlin', you are definitely of the softer-boiled variety."

"Isn't *The Last Clue* about the mob?"

"Yes, ma'am. Nicholas Post is hired by the mob boss to investigate a string of murders committed by rival gang members."

After arriving at the theater and picking up the reserved tickets, Larry bought two sodas, a big bucket of popcorn to share, and a movie magazine called *Inside the Silver Screen* that featured the very movie they were about to see.

Once seated, Rosa opened the magazine. "East Shore Productions Incorporated produced this film," she said. "It says here they are based in Boston."

"This movie is set there too, isn't it?" Larry said. "In 1912."

"Oh, I didn't realize the year!" Rosa looked closer at the article. "Aunt Louisa was born and raised there," Rosa said, "and though my mother was born in London, she grew up in Boston. She'd have lived there that year. I've never been to Boston, so I think I'm going to enjoy this!"

Larry draped an arm over Rosa's shoulder. "And I'm going to enjoy watching you enjoy it."

The theater darkened and the newsreels began: news that San Francisco's iconic cable line was being replaced by buses, and the winner of the Formula One Drivers' Championship.

"NASCAR is planning an exhibition race here in Santa Bonita," Larry said. "In November."

"Aunt Louisa mentioned that," Rosa returned. "One of her organizations is sponsoring it."

Dramatic music filled the theater as the credits began, and the moviegoers cheered. There was not a seat to spare, and it seemed much of Santa Bonita was excited to start watching.

As the movie progressed, the costumes of the times—the long stiff skirts worn by the women along with their modest long-sleeve blouses with high, button-up collars—intrigued Rosa. And the parasols and big hats could hardly have eased the summer heat. Rosa felt thankful to live in a time where a lady could wear a skirt that ended at the knees, and blouses with no sleeves at all!

But it was the setting of the city of Boston that interested Rosa the most. Boston Harbor differed greatly from Los Angeles on the Pacific Ocean, or London on the River Thames. Her mother had often talked about her transatlantic trip from Boston Harbor to Liverpool. That trip had been significant in several ways. It had been the first time that her mother, Ginger Gold, had met Rosa's father, Basil Reed, another passenger on the ship. It was also the first time Ginger had helped solve a murder with Basil leading the investigation.

Rosa owed her existence to that voyage. Had her mother never gone on that ship, Rosa would never have been born just a few years later. The ship had been called the SS *Rosa*—Rosa's namesake.

Every time the camera panned a shot of the city or the harbor, Rosa, fascinated with it all, leaned forward in her seat. Less impressive to Rosa, however, were the skills of some actors. The main villain in the movie, played by an actor named Scott Huntington, certainly looked the part with his dark, brooding good looks. Still, his acting seemed melodramatic, especially the scene where he was shot, which was a long, painfully dramatic affair causing Rosa to roll her eyes.

The magazine article hinted at a rivalry between this stuntman and Nicholas Post. *Was that actually true or something fabricated for publicity to promote the movie*, Rosa wondered.

"I'd put my money on the dark-haired feller in a real fistfight," Larry whispered in her ear as the two main characters brawled in an Irish pub. "Neither one of 'em seems to know how to operate a gun. They must've shot at each other at least a dozen times in that last scene, and no one got so much as a powder burn."

When the story reached the point where the private investigator rubbed a pencil across an old notepad to reveal hidden letters underneath, Rosa whispered back to Larry, "That's such an overused trick in detective stories. I've never once done that myself, and I doubt if any other detective ever has."

However, Rosa couldn't afford to be critical. Though she'd opened her office a couple of months earlier, business was slow. But she didn't want to think about that problem now and forced herself to focus on the film. Rosa realized that despite her critiques, she was pulled into the movie's plot and felt a sense of disappointment when the story ended.

As they stepped into the evening air and onto the sidewalk along with the rest of the movie patrons, Larry suggested drinks. "There's a bar just down the block."

"Yes, I would like that." Rosa linked her arm with his as they strolled down the street on a pleasantly cool evening.

While in her office the next morning, Rosa arranged the magazines on the teak coffee table for the third time. *Did the room look more welcoming now*? She'd placed an ad in the *Santa Bonita Gazette* that had garnered her a few new clients, but not enough to keep her mind and body busy.

She had worked at her mother's office, Lady Gold Investigations, in London. A long-running establishment—starting its operations since from before Rosa was born—Ginger Gold's business never hurt for clients. Her stellar reputation had been passed by word of mouth and hers was the first agency considered when most people needed a detective.

But how did one gain those qualities with a new business in Santa Bonita, California?

"What are we going to do, Diego?"

Rosa's brown tabby kitten, curled in the corner of the couch, feigned indifference to his owner's plight. He slowly closed his eyes and purred. Apparently, this new office space was even too boring for her cat.

A moment later, the door burst open, and there stood Gloria—all bright eyes and shiny red lipstick.

"Rosa! I thought I might find you here."

Gloria wore an emerald-green A-frame dress patterned with flecks of red and gold. A V-shaped neckline enhanced the capped sleeves. Around the creamy skin of her neck, a pearl choker hung, and her matching pearl belt emphasized her figure. Short curly hair framed her heart-shaped face, and although she'd tested a platinum-blonde look, her natural dark locks suited her much better.

Gloria waved the flyer in her hand. "Look what was posted on the bulletin board."

Rosa picked up on Gloria's infectious smile as she reached for the paper. *It might be a flyer advertising*

Reed Investigations, Rosa thought. However, her name and business were nowhere to be found on the flyer.

"Still a little slow?" Gloria asked, looking around the small office and stating the obvious. But Rosa's rapt attention was now fixed on the small white flyer.

It read: FILMING ON LOCATION IN SANTA BONITA, *QUICK STRIKE*—A WESTERN FILM BY DIRECTOR FREDERICK FORBES. EXTRAS NEEDED!

"That's intriguing," Rosa remarked. "If I'm not mistaken, that's the same director as last night's movie."

'It's the same director," Gloria confirmed. "Frederick Forbes is a very influential figure in that industry."

The qualifications for those who might be interested in extra work were listed under the heading. Prospective extras were people in their twenties with no distinguishing features such as scars or birthmarks on their faces. On the first day of filming, the possible extras had to be prepared to spend the first few hours going through the selection process, and then came makeup and wardrobe allocation.

Gloria came around Rosa and peered over her shoulder to read the flyer, even though Rosa couldn't imagine that her cousin hadn't already memorized every word. "It starts tomorrow," Gloria said. "I already asked if I could miss class—I thought the experience could be helpful." Gloria was a student at a local acting studio. She waved her hands around at the empty office. "It looks as though you're free too. Why don't you come with me?"

The idea of being in a movie—a Frederick Forbes film, no less—pumped more than a little extra adrenaline through Rosa's veins. It certainly beat rearranging coffee-table magazines all day while waiting for the telephone to ring.

"Rosa?" Gloria prodded. "You'll do it with me?"

"I don't know," Rosa hedged. "Acting isn't something I do well." She was purposely modest. In her line of work, she often had to pretend to be someone she wasn't.

Gloria pouted. "You don't have to act as an extra, not really. Anyway, I'll do all the work, you just have to respond to my cues." Gloria tugged on Rosa's arm. "Come on! It'll be fun!"

Rosa's hesitancy had nothing to do with acting, and she knew it. It had everything to do with a certain detective's fiancée, Charlene Winters, who Rosa knew would be on the set.

Rosa sat on the couch beside Diego and sorted out her crinolines and her emotions. Hadn't she carefully filed away her tumultuous romance with Miguel Belmonte into the past? Hadn't she been enjoying the time spent with her new boyfriend, the intelligent and respected Dr. Larry Rayburn, who had the prestigious position of assistant medical examiner?

Hadn't she *moved on*?

Rosa reached over to pet her kitten's soft fur. "What do you think, Diego? Can you live without me for a day?"

Diego's eyelids opened briefly but shut again as if the effort to look up at Rosa was too much. Rosa's mind spun quickly. Just because Charlene Winters would be on set, didn't mean she and Gloria would encounter the actress. Movie sets were notoriously busy places, and she knew she'd be one of many extras who milled about. *And what about Miguel*? Since he had his job to do at the Santa Bonita Police Department, there was no need to worry about him showing up.

Her choice was to while away the time in her office, hoping a client would call, or making her cousin happy.

She smiled up at Gloria. "Let's do it."

ABOUT THE AUTHORS

Lee Strauss is a USA TODAY bestselling author of The Ginger Gold Mysteries series, The Higgins & Hawke Mystery series, The Rosa Reed Mystery series (cozy historical mysteries), A Nursery Rhyme Mystery series (mystery suspense), The Perception series (young adult dystopian), The Light & Love series (sweet romance), The Clockwise Collection (YA time travel romance), and young adult historical fiction with over a million books read. She has titles published in German, Spanish and Korean, and a growing audio library.

When Lee's not writing or reading she likes to cycle, hike, and watch the ocean. She loves to drink caffè lattes and red wines in exotic places, and eat dark chocolate anywhere.

Norm Strauss is a singer-songwriter and performing artist who's seen the stage of The Voice of Germany. Short story writing is a new passion he shares with his wife Lee Strauss. Check out Norm's music page www.normstrauss.com

For more info on books by Lee Strauss and her social media links, visit leestraussbooks.com. To make sure you don't miss the next new release, be sure to sign up for her readers' list!

Did you know you can follow your favorite authors on Bookbub? If you subscribe to Bookbub — (and if you don't, why don't you? - They'll send you daily emails alerting you to sales and new releases on just the kind of books you like to read!) — follow me to make sure you don't miss the next Ginger Gold Mystery!

www.leestraussbooks.com
leestraussbooks@gmail.com

MORE FROM LEE STRAUSS

On AMAZON

THE ROSA REED MYSTERIES

(1950s cozy historical)

Murder at High Tide

Murder on the Boardwalk

Murder at the Bomb Shelter

Murder on Location

Murder and Rock 'n Roll

Murder at the Races

Murder at the Dude Ranch

Murder in London

Murder at the Fiesta

Murder at the Weddings

GINGER GOLD MYSTERY SERIES (cozy 1920s historical)

Cozy. Charming. Filled with Bright Young Things. This Jazz Age murder mystery will entertain and delight you with its 1920s flair and pizzazz!

Murder on the SS Rosa

Murder at Hartigan House

Murder at Bray Manor

Murder at Feathers & Flair

Murder at the Mortuary

Murder at Kensington Gardens

Murder at St. George's Church

The Wedding of Ginger & Basil

Murder Aboard the Flying Scotsman

Murder at the Boat Club

Murder on Eaton Square

Murder by Plum Pudding

Murder on Fleet Street

Murder at Brighton Beach

Murder in Hyde Park

Murder at the Royal Albert Hall

Murder in Belgravia

Murder on Mallowan Court

Murder at the Savoy

Murder at the Circus

Murder in France

Murder at Yuletide

LADY GOLD INVESTIGATES (Ginger Gold companion short stories)

Volume 1

Volume 2

Volume 3

Volume 4

HIGGINS & HAWKE MYSTERY SERIES (cozy 1930s historical)

The 1930s meets Rizzoli & Isles in this friendship depression era cozy mystery series.

Death at the Tavern

Death on the Tower

Death on Hanover

Death by Dancing

A NURSERY RHYME MYSTERY SERIES(mystery/sci fi)

Marlow finds himself teamed up with intelligent and savvy Sage Farrell, a girl so far out of his league he feels blinded in her presence - literally - damned glasses! Together they work to find the identity of @gingerbreadman. Can they stop the killer before he strikes again?

Gingerbread Man

Life Is but a Dream

Hickory Dickory Dock

Twinkle Little Star

LIGHT & LOVE (sweet romance)

Set in the dazzling charm of Europe, follow Katja, Gabriella, Eva, Anna and Belle as they find strength, hope and love.

Love Song

Your Love is Sweet

In Light of Us

Lying in Starlight

PLAYING WITH MATCHES (WW2 history/romance)

A sobering but hopeful journey about how one young German boy copes with the war and propaganda. Based on true events.

A Piece of Blue String (companion short story)

THE CLOCKWISE COLLECTION (YA time travel romance)

Casey Donovan has issues: hair, height and uncontrollable trips to the 19th century! And now this ~ she's accidentally taken Nate Mackenzie, the cutest boy in the school, back in time. Awkward.

Clockwise

Clockwiser

Like Clockwork

Counter Clockwise

Clockwork Crazy

Clocked (companion novella)

Standalones

Seaweed

Love, Tink

ACKNOWLEDGMENTS

Special thanks, as always, goes out to my editors Angelika Offenwanger, Robbie Bryant and Heather Belleguelle, along with my VIP readers Kelly Young and Polina Posner. I'm so glad you're enjoying Rosa Reed!

I can't forget my lovely assistant Shadi Bleiken (who is also my beautiful daughter in-law). Your competence and enthusiasm is a big part of my success as an indie writer. I'm so thankful for you!

And to Norm Strauss who's jumped into the world of Rosa Reed with both feet and is a master at 1950s trivia and historical events. I'm so happy to be doing this with you. Thank you for coming along on this crazy ride.

Printed in Poland
by Amazon Fulfillment
Poland Sp. z o.o., Wrocław